HIS ONE AND ONLY LADY

SECRETS OF SCANDALOUS LADIES
BOOK FOUR

COLLETTE CAMERON

For permission requests, write to the publisher at the address below.
Attn: Permissions Coordinator
info@collettecameronbooks.com
collettecameronbooks.com
eBook ISBN: 978-1-955259-17-0
Print Book ISBN: 978-1-966087-32-8

FREE BOOK!

JOIN MY EXCLUSIVE MAILING LIST
Collette Cameron Newsletter

AND GET A FREE EBOOK!

https://collettecameronbooks.com/freegift

Plus Sneak Peeks, Giveaways, Contests, Exclusive Content, and More... P.S. I promise only good stuff ~ **no** spam!

you read it when you can read it all. You will not want to put it down." ~ *Sherry Tritt Holton*

★★★★★ "This is a lovely story that pulled me in from the beginning. There are secrets and scandals, but there is also heartwarming romance that will charm you and put a smile on your face." ~ *Sahar's Honest Reviews*

★★★★★ "This is a lovely story with more absolutely wonderful characters than you can count (a few not-so-wonderful ones as well). I happily recommend it (and a visit to a secret garden)." ~ PeggyC51

For the introverts who prefer to people watch rather than talk at gatherings, whose idea of a fantastic evening is staying home and reading a book, and who make the best friends because though it takes them a while to open up, they remain loyal for a lifetime.

ACKNOWLEDGMENTS

This is my fifty-first historical romance. What a journey it has been from that day in February 2011 when I sat before a computer and started writing my first book.

My immediate family deserves more thanks than I can express for their patience as I infamously said countless times, "I have to finish this book."

I am so grateful to my loyal readers who faithfully rush out to buy my new releases, respond to my newsletters, and especially my Cheris in my Facebook reader group. So many of you have become good friends and brought so much joy to my life.

I have to acknowledge my incredible, dedicated reviewers who selflessly give of their time by reviewing my books and providing me with invaluable feedback. Your commitment humbles and blesses me.

Lastly, but certainly not least, I must thank my assistants. Without you, I would never have the time to write as much as I do. You keep me organized, and I know I can rely on you for the dozens of things that unexpectedly come my way.

Here's to another fifty books over the next ten years.

That man is an ogre!

What an impossible predicament you find yourself in, Faith. I know how much you anticipated your new position as an amanuensis for Lord Kellinggrave. He only retained you because he lost a wager, you say? I do believe his lordship is a despicable knave for misleading you.

For what it is worth, I applaud your intrepidness and gumption. Do not let the scapegrace chase you away. I know you, Faith, and you shall make an excellent scrivener. His lordship shall learn as much if he puts aside his masculine prejudices.

I hope to visit you and Chasity, Joy, Mercy, and Faith soon. My tenure with the Ceddes family is ending as Pomeroy is off to Harrow and the girls to boarding school this autumn—the poor dears. After eight years, I've grown very fond of the children and shall miss them dreadfully.

But alas, time ticks relentlessly onward, and I must search for a new position even while I'm at the Mumfords' house party. I shall pray I never have an employer as impossible as your Lord Kellinggrave.

~Miss Purity Mayfield, in a letter written
en route to the Mumfords'
to Miss Faith Roth

Mottford Hall, Essex, England
Home of the Earl and Countess of Mumford
22 August 1818 — Mid-Morning

Bliss. Pure, sublime bliss.

Purity Mayfield tilted her face into the sun's soothing rays and gave a contented sigh. Humming the ballad she'd sung to her wards that morning, she relaxed into the comfortable, cushioned chaise lounge—one of several in the cozy garden. Apparently, none of the other houseguests who'd arrived over the past couple of days had discovered this magical retreat yet.

To be honest, she wasn't exactly one of the elite *haut ton* guests. Nevertheless, she felt as privileged as one at that moment. Glancing around the isolated enclosure, Purity smiled.

Her cherished privacy might be partially due to the ten-foot-tall beech hedge surrounding the charming square and its distance from the manor house. She'd accidentally come upon the hedgerow's arched opening while walking the greens farthest from the opulent mansion.

A few feet from her, across the verdant grass paralleled by rust-colored brick pavers lay a square pond. An angel wearing a strategically placed loincloth for modesty's sake topped a two-tiered burbling fountain.

For the moment, this enchanted haven was all hers to enjoy. No quieting energetic children, wiping noses, gently but firmly reminding her charges to mind their manners, or doing the often unreasonable bidding of her employers.

For a few coveted minutes, it was just Purity, the fish, a few bees, and a mild August morning sun.

She eyed the entrance with a mixture of trepidation and expectation.

Surely this heaven was too perfect to last.

The reluctance of the upper ten thousand to part with their plush mattresses before noon also likely explained why no others had joined her in this picturesque retreat.

That was perfectly fine with Purity.

More than fine, in truth.

In general, the upper class had little use for servants except how the menials made their elite lives more comfortable and convenient. Respect, consideration, and basic politeness were reserved for those of the same social standing as members of *le beau monde*—not the lower orders.

As a governess, Purity fell somewhere between the servants and the family she worked for. She wasn't included in either, and it made for a rather lonely existence—apart from her time with the children in her charge.

As accomplished as she was at appearing subservient and compliant, there were moments she had to bite the inside of her cheek to keep her ungracious opinions to herself or stifle a disrespectful, if honest, retort.

Her current employers, the Viscount and Viscountess Ceddes, were challenging on the best day and intolerable on a bad one. She'd long since learned to recite in her head, "a soft answer turneth away wrath," over and over.

Never mind how much *she* might fume after a disagreeable encounter. Her position, and thus her future, depended on an acquiescent and submissive demeanor.

Neither trait came naturally to her.

She'd often wondered if either of her parents—she had no idea who they might be—had possessed a tenacious nature too. Or which she'd inherited her riot of curly hair from.

Shading her eyes with her hand, Purity spied a squirrel cautiously creeping across the grass. Sitting on its haunches, it darted its black-eyed gaze here and there, its tiny little nose twitching all the while. The darling thing would advance a couple of feet, flick its fluffy red tail, and repeat its anxious perusal.

Perhaps it drank from the fountain daily.

Purity lowered her hand, and the squirrel dashed into the hedge. A second later, it poked its head out and scolded her for her audacity.

She chuckled. "I'll be gone soon, my little friend. Let me enjoy these few stolen moments in paradise before my world returns to normal."

Drumming her fingertips on the chaise's arms, Purity permitted her mind to return to her earlier reflections. To be fair, disagreeable interactions with Lord and Lady Ceddes had been infrequent since they seldom deemed it necessary to visit their offspring.

Attending this house party was an unofficial send-off for Pomeroy, Merrilee, and Amaris Bardslay. It was also the longest expanse of time the couple had spent with their children since they'd hired Purity. Neither parent demonstrated paternal inclinations. Ten minutes with their offspring stretched the bounds of their benevolence.

In just over four short weeks, Purity's charges would be off to boarding schools, and she would be unemployed for the first time since leaving Haven House and Academy for the Enrichment of Young Women—the foundling home and school where she'd been raised and educated.

Hopefully, she'd manage a visit with a few of her closest

friends, also raised at Haven House and Academy for the Enrichment of Young Women, before she started her new job.

A job she'd yet to acquire, as she had no letter of reference yet.

She'd waited for months—growing increasingly impatient —for her employers to offer to write her a recommendation or even mention that, very shortly, her services would no longer be required. They'd remained frustratingly obtuse and disobliging in that regard. Now, she found herself in the discomfiting position of having to ask for a reference while in attendance at this house party.

She made a dismissive sound in her throat.

Enough of this unfruitful, melancholy musing.

With deliberate intent, Purity turned her thoughts in a more pleasant direction: this glorious, unforeseen reprieve from responsibilities. She'd been given an unexpected gift, and she meant to enjoy every splendid second.

After breakfast, Lady Ceddes had actually collected her children for a morning outing with several other families and didn't require Purity's services for a few hours.

Would wonders never cease?

There *was* a first time for everything.

Purity gave a slight shake of her head, and a curl flopped loose from her chignon.

Dratted nuisance.

An unremarkable light brown, her hair had vexed her since girlhood when she'd been required to wrestle the unruly mass into a neat knot by Hester Shepherd, the headmistress at Haven House and Academy for the Enrichment of Young Women.

Once Purity had captured the strand fluttering about her face in the fragrant honeysuckle and rose-scented breeze, she confined the wayward curl with a pin. Giving her hair a satisfied pat to ensure no more intrepid tresses were about to spring loose, she settled into the luxurious chaise lounge once more.

She determined nothing would stir her from her current contentment.

When was the last time she'd had an entire morning to herself?

At Petherwick Court, the Ceddes primary estate in Somerset, a myriad of tasks always needed attending to if the children were engaged elsewhere. Governesses of three energetic children seldom were permitted such a luxury. Governesses to self-centered aristocrats such as her employers, who seldom saw their offspring, even less so.

And yet here she was. Unfettered by her three charges and without a single duty to perform. In all of her eight years employed by the Ceddes, this was a first. A most pleasant and welcome first, indeed.

Crossing her ankles, Purity grinned, feeling very much a pampered lady of leisure.

The sensation was both disconcerting and delightful.

She wiggled her toes in her practical black half boots and furrowed her brow at the frayed hem of her slate blue gown. Now wasn't the time to add to her scant wardrobe. Best to wait until she found a new position and then acquire an appropriate new gown or two.

Drowsy from the sun's warmth, the comforting buzz of engorged gold and ebony bees zipping from fat blossom to even fatter blossom, and the sweet warbles of songbirds, she permitted her eyelids to drift shut.

Awaking with a start, she snapped her gaping mouth closed and touched a fingertip to the side of her mouth to catch the unladylike dribble of drool perched there. Goodness, she'd been far more tired than she'd realized. Thank the Lord there hadn't been anyone about to see her lack of decorum.

Furrowing her brow, she glanced around.

What had awakened her?

She'd heard something. Something—no, *someone*—in distress.

Head cocked, she listened keenly past the sounds of the frothing fountain, humming bees, and chirping birds.

There.

A faint sniffle and a muffled sob.

Rising, Purity perused the square enclosure.

Nothing.

Another pitiful sob cut through the garden's tranquility.

The thread of sound came from near the entrance.

Did someone hide in one of the nooks created by the zealously tended beeches on either side of the tapered arc? Purity had been so entranced with this oasis that she'd scarcely paid the weathered stone benches nestled there any mind when she'd stumbled upon the secret garden.

Swiftly making her way across the expanse, her shoes and skirts swishing against the short grass as she went, she approached the opening. As she neared the entrance, Purity slowed her pace when she spied a little girl's tousled red hair.

At the dejected little form huddled there, Purity's heart wrenched, and she pressed a hand to her bosom.

Dear Lord. The poor darling.

TWO

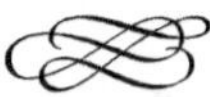

Theran, you and Bernadine must attend our house party in August. I've invited several families with young children so she'll have playmates to occupy her time while you join in the adult activities. Most of the guests with children are bringing their governesses as well, and with the extra maids I've retained for the month, there is no need for you to concern yourself with Bernadine's care.

I shan't take no for an answer, Nephew. Imogene has been gone for almost three years. It's time you started living again, my dear. I'd prefer you didn't bring that creature with you, even if Athena has been acting as a quasi-nurse and governess for the dear child these past months. I suppose I can make an allowance if you cannot discourage Athena's attendance, but do endeavor to put her off. She'll cast a pall over the festivities.

How very different Imogene was from Athena, but then again, they were stepsisters.

~Melvelia Hawtrey, Countess of Mumford,
in an invitation to her nephew,

Mister Theran Rutland

Mottford Hall's Secret Garden
A few heartbeats later

The child had pulled her feet onto the bench, her petite white shoes peeking from the hem of her gown. Knees tucked to her chest, the girl had buried her head in her thin arms atop her knees and wept as if her heart were broken. She couldn't have been more than three or four years old.

"Where *are* you, Bernadine?" a woman asked in the distance, her tone harsh but refined. "Answer me this minute, or I shall punish you most severely."

Bernadine?

Purity's attention rested on the miserable waif for a moment before returning to the opening. Given the toddler's fashionable yellow gown and white stockings and shoes, she was likely quality.

"Rotten little bratling," the woman snapped with enough venom to raise Purity's nape hair. "I ought to let you stay out here and get good and lost. It's no more than an ugly, miserable, motherless urchin like you deserves."

God above, what a nasty termagant.

Unfamiliar outrage, instant and searing, burgeoned behind Purity's breast bone.

Who was this vindictive woman?

How dare she speak to a child so cruelly?

Purity crouched before the child and tenderly touched her shoulder.

"Bernadine?"

Gasping, the little girl raised her tear-ravaged face. Huge, soulful green eyes, red-rimmed from weeping, gazed at her in shock and alarm. Her mouth opened in a silent cry, and she jerked away, cowering in the corner.

"It's all right, dear. I shan't hurt you. I promise," Purity soothed in the same manner she had the two wild kittens a mama cat had deserted in the stables at Petherwick Court. Plump kittens, which now led a luxurious and pampered life in Petherwick Court. Smiling, she gently pushed a strand of damp red hair off Bernadine's cheek.

"Is she your mama?" Purity asked, praying that wasn't the case.

"No! *No!*" Bernadine whispered raggedly while giving a vehement shake of her coppery head. "But she wants to be. Then she'll send me to a bored..." Forehead furrowed, she screwed her bow-shaped lips together. "To bord-ded school, far, *far* away."

So, that was the way of it then. Boarding school for this poor child.

Did Bernadine's father know how dreadfully the woman treated his daughter? Once again, Purity sent up a short prayer that he had no idea how contemptibly the woman who thought to become his wife treated his daughter.

It mightn't be her place, and she'd be stepping over the mark, but impertinent or not, Purity fully intended to advise him of what she had overheard.

When she found out *who* he was.

Lower lip quivering, the child cut such a fearful glance toward the opening, Purity's heart lurched once more.

What kind of monster had terrified this little girl so?

When Bernadine turned her face away, Purity spied the clear, angry red outline of a palm upon the little girl's peach skin. An adult palm print.

Another wave of ire sluiced through her.

"I'm Purity, Bernadine. You can trust me. I shall keep you safe."

For the next few minutes, but then what?

Surely any father, upon learning how despicably the woman had spoken to his child, would protect his offspring from further abuse.

"*Bern-a-dine?*" the woman called again, her angry voice grating like coach wheels upon gravel.

Bernadine remained stonily silent with her fearful gaze riveted on the garden entrance.

"Fine, you horrid little red-haired daughter of the devil," the woman ranted. "I'll explain to your father how you've been disobedient and insolent again. Perhaps being locked in your room for another three days, with only bread and water, will teach you to respect your betters."

She locked the child in her room and only fed her bread and water?

Where in Hades was the child's father when this occurred?

"I wasn't dis-bead-inet or solent," Bernadine mumbled, pushing her lower lip out and glowering. "That's a lie." She peeped up at Purity, obviously still uncertain she could trust her. "Papa says liars are the devil's mouf-peach."

Mouthpiece?

Hiding a smile at the child's adorable mispronunciations, Purity quite agreed with that assessment.

"Your papa is a very wise man."

Nodding, Bernadine sniffled and rubbed her reddened nose on her forearm. "Aunt Athena said she was going to be my mama. I said she wasn't, so she slapped me."

That appalling woman was the child's aunt? And wanted to be her mother?

Heaven forbid.

It took all of Purity's restraint to quell the ugly retort that throttled to the back of her teeth. Nonetheless, several unflattering descriptions of the woman tumbled around her brain. A few downright vulgar ones as well that would've sent dear Mrs. Shepherd into a swoon had any of her pupils ever voiced something so uncouth and unladylike.

"Here." Purity pulled an embroidered handkerchief from her pocket.

Any governess worth her salt kept at least three fresh handkerchiefs on hand. She would've tended to the child's nose and face herself, but as they were strangers and Bernadine was distrustful, Purity deemed it wiser to let the imp try herself.

Bernadine accepted the cloth, her lips tilting up at the corners at the bluebird in the corner. "A birdy. It's pretty."

"It is." Purity bent her mouth into an encouraging arch. "Wipe your face and nose. You won't harm it."

Bernadine did as bid and then bashfully held out the crumpled square. "Thank you."

The child had pretty manners.

"You are most welcome." Purity accepted the wadded cloth and tucked it into her empty pocket. A trick she'd learned long ago.

Right pocket—clean handkerchiefs. Left pocket—soiled ones.

Listening intently for anyone's approach, Purity considered the situation.

She had no idea who the woman searching for Bernadine was, but immediate and profound dislike had sprung up inside her for the mean-spirited creature.

Was she one of the houseguests?

Was Bernardine?

"Who is your father, Bernadine? What is his name?"

Bernadine turned her spiky-lashed emerald-green eyes on

Purity. Love and admiration promptly filled her innocent gaze. "Papa."

"Yes, he is Papa to you, but what name do others address him by, dearest?"

Screwing her face in concentration, Bernadine stared at her fingers entwined in her lap. She suddenly brightened. "Theran. Aunt Athena calls him Theran. Mrs. Spraggs—she's our cook and makes yummy tarts—calls him Mr. Rutland."

Theran Rutland.

Not a peer if his staff addressed him as mister.

Purity didn't know him, but that wasn't a surprise. She knew few of the people the Mumfords had invited to their annual country house party.

"Shall we search for your papa together?" She held out her hand. "I promise to keep you safe until we find him."

Even from that witch out there.

Head canted, Bernadine stared at Purity for a long, assessing moment. At last, as if Purity had passed some sort of silent test, the child nodded and extended her tiny hand as she hopped off the bench.

The show of trust warmed Purity's heart.

Now, where to begin the search for her father?

They exited the hedgerow, and Purity skimmed her gaze over the area, looking for the hateful woman. Several guests wandered the greens in the distance, but no one—especially a spiteful female—stomped about nearby.

Or flew about on her broom.

Thank goodness, because this time Purity wasn't sure she'd be able to bridle her tongue. The harpy might find herself on the receiving end of a tongue lashing like nothing she'd ever experienced before.

As they slowly walked toward the impressive manor house, four stories of windows sparkling in the sunlight,

Purity asked, "Are you and your papa here for the Mumfords' house party?"

Nodding, Bernadine wrinkled her little nub of a nose and pulled a face. "Aunt Athena too. I was hiding from her."

After Purity told Theran Rutland what she'd overheard, he'd have to be a numbskull to entertain any notion of marrying that horrid woman. Purity pointedly disregarded the nagging voice that whispered her impertinence might not be well received.

Or if Mr. Rutland complained to the Ceddes, she could lose her position.

She would be without employment soon anyway.

Shrugging, she strode onward.

In for a penny, in for a pound.

THREE

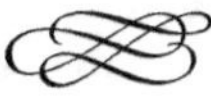

I hope my letter finds you well. Though I was offered the headmistress position at Balderbrook's Institution for Genteel Ladies, as I was betrothed, I declined to accept. However, I believe there are still positions at the school that have not been filled. I would be happy to use my influence to recommend you as an instructor when your tenure at Petherwick Court ends. You've only to ask me.

I would also like to invite you for an extended visit when you leave your current employer. I am sending this missive to Petherwick Court, as I don't know who is hosting the house party you mentioned in your last letter. I hope it is forwarded to you in a timely fashion.

~ Chasity Terramier, in a letter
to Purity Mayfield

Mottford Hall's Lawns
A scant few seconds later

The tightness in Theran's chest eased upon spying his daughter holding hands with a young woman as they ambled across the neatly trimmed lawn. Other than a slightly rumpled gown, Bernadine looked no worse for wear.

"Bernadine," he said, to himself, his tone underscored with relief. "There you are."

He nodded to Grayson Hemsworth and Devin Everingham, longtime friends from their days at Oxford together, as he traversed the pathways adorned with various topiaries along the formal lawns near the house.

He took a second look at the closest figure.

Was that supposed to be a dog?

Mayhap a pig?

In the distance, a cow lowed, and a rook cawed as it flew by overhead with something in its beak.

Having searched the house for several minutes already, Theran had grown increasingly concerned when he couldn't locate Bernadine. Real panic had clawed at his spine when he'd been unable to find her.

After sending a pair of maids to continue to comb the manor inside and asking Kebble, the butler, to notify him if Bernadine was found, Theran had taken to the grounds.

Sunlight glinted off Bernadine's shiny, coppery hair, so much like her mother's fiery tresses. Familiar melancholy kicked behind Theran's breastbone.

Lord, how he'd adored Imogene's flaming tresses. Her shrewd wit and contagious laugh. Even her occasional fiery scolds. Their three blissful years together had been cut short when she'd fallen ill with what had started as a simple cold.

He quickened his pace, eager to assure himself Bernadine was as unharmed as she appeared. She was the most important thing in his life, and he couldn't help the surge of annoyance toward his stepsister-in-law, Athena Sommerville, that he found himself fraught with worry the first day of this house party.

What would Imogene think?

That Theran was failing to live up to his promises?

God knew he was trying.

His last words to his cherished wife as she lay dying were a promise to keep their daughter safe. That she'd never be foisted off on nurses or governesses and that Bernadine would know how much her mother and father loved her.

Striding across the verdant lawns, his boots sinking into the lush grass, he permitted his mouth to bend upward.

As was Bernadine's wont, she *hop-hop-hopped* three times toward him.

Her companion, a woman unremarkable in appearance and dress, smiled at his daughter's antics. The woman said something to Bernadine he couldn't make out because of their distance. Whatever she'd said made Bernadine glance up, grin, and nod before hopping forward again.

Warmth infused him this stranger's patience toward his energetic daughter, so *very* much like her spirited mother. He could never quash Bernadine's enthusiasm or joy for life, even if it meant she didn't always display the decorum and politesse the *ton* preferred.

Theran had been on the cusp of asking his hosts to send a few footmen to also look for Bernadine. When he'd finally seen her, a surge of relief had left him slightly dizzy. Not that Bernadine was lost when an adult accompanied her. But she could easily have been.

Or worse, wandered to the small lake—where even now, a quartet of skiffs bobbed—and fallen in. Bernadine didn't know how to swim. As Atherley Hall's lands also contained a large pond, she needed to learn and soon. Theran had meant to teach her, but time had slipped away from him.

He put two fingers to his temple as he marched along. How could it be that Bernadine would celebrate her fourth birthday in October?

Glancing over his shoulder toward the house, he scanned the guests milling about the terrace and lawns.

Still no Athena.

Where was she?

After all, she insisted on accompanying him and Bernadine, even though he'd politely—quite firmly in truth— tried to put her off. Either Athena was as obtuse as a turnip to his numerous hints, or she was simply mulish. He'd come to believe the latter. Still, he couldn't very well tell her Aunt Melvelia had expressly asked that Athena not come.

Regardless, she should've been outside searching for Bernadine as he had been. But she wasn't, which made him once again regret agreeing to allow her to take on the role of Bernadine's caregiver.

When he'd returned from his early morning ride a short time ago, he'd encountered Athena in the foyer, flustered and put-upon. She claimed Bernadine had run off after having a tantrum, and she'd been looking for her ever since.

Neither behavior was typical for Bernadine, but according to his sister-in-law, Bernadine had become difficult to manage of late. Particularly when business called him away. He had an easy solution for that. Next time, he'd take Bernadine with him, but he'd have to hire a governess first.

Though he didn't like being apart from his daughter, Theran had been in London for the past three weeks on business. Rather, attending a series of meetings regarding the production and harvesting of crops as well as new fertilization methods. As a gentleman farmer, he was intrigued with introducing modern farming techniques.

He firmly believed England's agricultural future depended upon it.

That had required him to be away from his beloved daughter, and according to Athena, Bernadine had been contrary, disobedient, and disrespectful in his absence.

Eight months ago, when Bernadine's nurse had unexpectedly married, Athena had volunteered to come to stay at Atherley Hall and *temporarily* act as Bernadine's nurse and governess. Initially, Theran had thought it charitable of his wife's stepsister and that it might do Bernadine well to have her aunt nearby.

That assessment had changed in the months since.

Every time he suggested it was time to search for a permanent replacement, Athena found one excuse or another to delay his hiring a nurse and governess. Of late, a possessive glint in her eye had made him wary. The change he'd observed in Bernadine in recent weeks concerned him the most. He'd have to be blind and addlepated to not notice his daughter didn't like Athena.

Bernadine was too polite to say as much but shrank into herself whenever Athena spoke to her.

The question was, why?

He'd have that answer sooner rather than later.

In truth, it was far past time his sister-in-law returned home. People had already begun to speculate about their relationship. He'd heard a few whispers while in London recently, and Aston Terramier had told him bluntly of the ugly tattle. Rumors abounded that Theran and Athena were lovers, and marriage wasn't far off for the pair.

Not a raindrop's chance in a fire of that happening. If Theran had wanted to marry Athena, he'd have done so rather than wed her younger-by-five-years stepsister Imogene.

No, Athena must go. She should never have stayed this long.

He was a fool for allowing her to come when every instinct had screamed for him not to.

"I've been looking everywhere for you, my dear," Theran said when he was within hearing distance of Bernadine.

The woman accompanying his daughter released Bernadine's hand.

Who was she, and why was his daughter with her?

Her simple, unadorned gown suggested she might be a companion to an elderly dame or perhaps governess to one of the families who'd also brought their children to the Mumfords' annual house party.

"Papa!"

Bernadine's face illuminated with a joyous smile. She dashed toward him, her tousled locks bouncing and pirouetting as her little legs churned.

Squatting to embrace her, Theran captured her in a warm hug. As he rose with her in his arms, he kissed her forehead. "I was worried about you, little rabbit."

Cook had given Bernadine the nickname a couple of years ago because she loved to hop around, pretending to be a bunny. She now owned a fluffy black-and-white bunny of her very own named Princess Hoppy.

For what else would a little girl name her pet bunny?

Bernadine smiled up at him, her green, green eyes so jubilant, he couldn't help but return the smile even as concern rooted around his mind.

If he didn't miss his mark, she'd been crying. Her eyelashes were still spiky and her cheeks flushed—one quite red in truth. He'd have the reason why from the woman waiting patiently, hands clasped before her plain blue gown and head slightly angled as she observed the reunion.

She possessed a subtle regal dignity, an effortless elegance that bespoke aristocratic heritage. Mayhap, she, like so many unfortunates, had fallen on hard times and been forced to make their way in this unkind world.

Now wasn't the time to scold Bernadine for running off. Especially as he hadn't heard her side of the story. He'd never known Bernadine to lie.

Half-turning in his arms, she waved toward the woman, standing a few feet away.

"Purty, this is my papa."

He took the woman's measure from the top of her head to the black tips of her well-worn but polished half boots. Upon closer inspection, the woman was rather pretty in an unassuming way.

She approached him, and Theran found himself looking into eyes almost as green as Bernadine's. Where Bernadine's were a clear emerald, this woman's were a turbulent ocean green.

A hint of something—trepidation?

No, by Jove. *Reproach* shadowed her gaze.

He scowled.

Who was *she* to find fault with *him*?

High cheekbones and winged almond-brown eyebrows accented the delicate planes of her oval face. Her creamy skin, plum-colored lips, and dark fan of eyelashes needed no cosmetics to enhance them. According to *le beau monde* standards, she was no great beauty, but neither had Imogene been.

His daughter's rescuer possessed inviting features with the merest hint of mystery. As if something more went on behind those lustrous eyes in direct contrast to the calm deportment she presented. Undeterred by Theran's disapproving glare, she met his gaze directly, sharp intelligence in hers.

"Mr. Rutland. I am Purity Mayfield. I came across your

daughter hiding in an enclosed garden." She angled her slender form toward a tall row of beeches on the far side of the estate grounds and gave a graceful flick of her hand. "Over there. There's a secret garden of sorts, not easily detectable unless you are directly in front of it."

Bernadine had been clear out there by herself?

Miss Mayfield met his gaze again, hers brimming with expectation.

Theran smothered his earlier annoyance at her judging him. She had found Bernadine and brought her safely to him, after all.

"I thank you, Miss Mayfield, for returning my daughter to me." He glanced downward to Bernadine's mop of ginger curls. Love for her constricted his throat momentarily. "She is my everything."

Miss Mayfield's eyes went soft at the edges, and something shifted in the depths of her eyes. Theran swore genuine fondness colored her expression when she gravitated her attention to Bernadine.

Bernadine wrapped her arms around his neck and laid her cheek against his chest. "Papa, I like Purty better than Aunt Athena. Can she be my mama instead?"

Miss Mayfield made a choking sound even as an involuntary noise echoed in Theran's throat.

He raised his startled glance to Miss Mayfield's, prepared to offer an apology, but stopped with his mouth parted.

Her expression had grown taut—no, thunderous—and fire all but sparked in her marine-green irises.

"Might I have a word with you in private, Mr. Rutland?"

Her request was perfectly composed, but a thread of steel edged her question.

Few women in service dared such impertinence.

An uneasy sensation tiptoed across Theran's shoulders.

"As we are unacquainted, might I inquire why?" He kissed Bernadine's crown, enjoying holding her. Soon she'd be too big to do so.

She smelled of lemon and cinnamon.

"It's regarding something I overheard." Miss Mayfield's gaze settled on Bernadine again. "Something I believe you should be made aware of."

She'd chosen her words with care, but Theran couldn't shake the instinct that she referred to Bernadine.

He was already late for the game of cricket he'd been coerced into playing by Everingham and Hemsworth. Nonetheless, courtesy dictated he hear what Miss Mayfield had to say.

Nodding, he adjusted Bernadine in his arms. "I know the house well, as it is my aunt and uncle's. We can be assured of privacy in my aunt's personal salon. Please allow me to return Bernadine to my sister-in-law's care—"

"*No, Papa. No!*" Bernadine buried her face in his neck and tightened her hold around his neck so tight that she nearly strangled him. "Please don't make me go with her. *Ple-ase,*" she said in a tormented whisper.

Tension throttled through Theran.

My God. What had happened to terrify Bernadine so?

"That is what I wish to speak with you about." Miss Mayfield's attention shifted to behind him, and her features tightened even more. Her pretty eyes narrowed in a distinct challenge, and she pulled her full mouth into a prim, disapproving line.

"You've found her, Theran," Athena said behind him in dulcet tones.

He turned as she approached.

Her pale pink gown, sprinkled with tiny white rosebuds, complemented her fair beauty. She knew it too, from the manner in which she postured. "Thank the Lord, the darling is all right."

FOUR

You must use whatever means necessary to get Theran to propose, daughter. It's been eight months since you moved to Atherley Hall. Whatever is taking so long? I know you cannot abide that child, but once you're wed, she can be sent to a school in Switzerland until she's of marriageable age.

Our financial straits have become most dire. Dire, I tell you!

Creditors are threatening us with debtor's prison. I vow, your stepfather doesn't have the business sense of a beetle anymore. All of those imprudent investments... What a fool I was to marry him for financial security. The old fraud was not as plush in the pockets as I'd been led to believe.

He's not been the same since Imogene's death, and you and I must take matters into our own hands. If you must, get Theran drunk and seduce him. He's a man. They all are barbarians under their starched neckcloths.

I needn't remind you that you're not getting any younger, and your prospects are dismal without a dowry.

You're clever and cunning, Athena. After all, you're my daughter.

Do what you must, and do it quickly.

~Mrs. Albertina Bambrick, in a letter
to her daughter, Athena Sommerville

Still on the Mumfords' lawn
Fifteen extremely uncomfortable seconds later

For the first time in Purity's life, she itched to slap another person. Hands clenched until her nails bit into her palms, she forced herself to take a deep, stabilizing breath and gripped her composure firmly. That didn't stop her from wishing the good Lord would smite Athena whatever-her-surname-was into ashes.

She'd repent for her uncharitable thoughts when she said her evening prayers.

In point of fact, as incensed as Purity was, it might take several bouts of prayer to get the job done properly. Thankfully, the Lord was merciful and forgiving if one repented.

That might be the greater challenge, in truth.

"Miss Mayfield, permit me to introduce my sister-in-law, Miss Athena Sommerville. Athena has graciously acted as Bernadine's nurse and governess until I hire a replacement for her former nurse."

Not his betrothed then.

Thank God.

The fabric of Mr. Rutland's navy-blue riding coat pulled taut across his broad shoulders as he angled toward his sister-in-law. He towered over her, and even Purity, considered tall for a woman at five feet nine inches herself, had to look up to meet his probing gaze. The sun glinted off his raven hair as he drew his hawkish eyebrows together over an aquiline nose.

Inarguably handsome, Mr. Rutland also bore an air of disenchantment—or perhaps *cynicism* better described him.

Why Purity should care so much about a child she just met or that the little girl's father was not affianced to Miss Sommerville escaped rationale. Or why she should poke her nose into another family's business.

And yet, there she was. Doing precisely that.

Miss Sommerville twisted her mouth into a semblance of a brittle smile. She'd not liked Mr. Rutland clarifying her position. From the annoyance she struggled vainly to hide, not at all.

Purity filed those interesting facts into a corner of her mind.

"Athena, may I present Miss Purity Mayfield. She found Bernadine and was in the process of bringing her to the house when I came upon them."

An insincere smile stretching her face, Miss Sommerville tilted her artfully coiffed blond head in what she no doubt believed was a regal angle, but which instead made her look as if she had a painful crick in her neck. "How fortuitous for everyone."

Purity didn't miss the shrewd assessment in the woman's brown eyes or the way she sidled to Mr. Rutland's side and laid a possessive hand on the forearm cradling his daughter.

She might as well have bared her teeth and hissed, "*He's mine. Stay away.*"

Purity gave the barest inclination of her head in greeting. Never had she been so impolite, but this woman...this, this *creature*... Nay. Athena Sommerville, for all of her outward beauty, didn't deserve civility.

The planes of his chiseled face taking on a flinty edge, Mr.

Rutland looked between Purity and the new arrival. A warning flashed in his indigo eyes beneath his slanted midnight eyebrows.

Did he object to her impoliteness?

Well, why shouldn't he?

Purity had been rude. A first for her, and the feeling was quite novel.

Theran Rutland was no dimwit, however. From the keen way he assessed her and Miss Sommerville, he obviously sensed the tense undercurrent.

"Yes, Bernadine is fine," he said at last, wrapping his arms more securely around his daughter and dislodging Miss Sommerville's hand.

Deliberately.

Unless Purity was mistaken, and she very much thought she was not.

Now, wasn't that an interesting turn and a wholly welcome one too.

It only confirmed that Purity wouldn't be telling an infatuated man his future wife was a hateful and abusive monster.

A frown of irritation furrowed Miss Sommerville's countenance before she swiftly arranged her features into such serene tranquility, one might believe her Madonna act. Except, Purity had heard what this shrew was capable of with her own ears.

"I am so very relieved," Miss Sommerville purred, gazing at Bernadine with contrived adoration.

What a brilliant actress.

She'd missed her calling, by George. Miss Sommerville should've taken to the stage.

For her part, Bernadine kept her head tucked into her father's shoulder and refused to look at her aunt as they neared the terrace.

"Well, after all of this excitement, I'm sure Bernadine is ready for a nap, aren't you, my dear?" Miss Sommerville touched Bernadine's leg, and the child flinched and pulled away.

Mr. Rutland blue eyes darkened to navy-blue and narrowed minutely at the edges.

He'd seen his daughter's reaction.

Good.

Purity's initial assessment of him had been correct. He was astute and observant. Apparently, he was a loving father, too, from her brief observation.

As they neared the terrace doors, Lady Mumford and her youngest daughter, Forsythia, exited. Both females wore vibrant, multicolored gowns, generously swathed in layer upon layer of bows, ruffles, and lace. The effect was...unforgettable.

The countess's other daughters, eighteen-year-old Delphine and sixteen-year-old Amaryllis, tended to wear equally generously adorned gowns. In point of fact, the three daughters, named for flowers, often resembled blossoms themselves.

A genuine smile of affection crumpled Lady Mumford's plump features as her eyes lit with pleasure. The startling array of feathers in her chignon perfectly matched the cobalt blue, primrose yellow, and fuchsia gown stretched over her generous curves. "Ah, Theran. Forsythia was just asking if she might show Bernadine the puppies in the stables."

Forsythia aptly wore a bright yellow gown, but her tangerine and raspberry striped spencer did nothing to complement her spotty teenage complexion.

Bernadine lifted her head, excitement shining in her eyes. "May I, Papa? Please?"

A fond smile softened the angular contours of Mr.

Rutland's face. "Of course, pet. But you have to promise to take your nap afterward without any fuss."

"I promise." Bernadine gave an eager nod. "I shall go straight to sleep."

He set her down, and her cousin clasped her hand.

"I'll take good care of her, Theran," his pretty, young cousin, still harboring a hint of baby fat, assured him before leading Bernadine away.

Hop. Hop. Hop.

Bernadine giggled as she hopped along.

"Excuse me a moment while I have a word with my aunt, please." Mr. Rutland took his aunt's elbow and guided her a few feet away, where they spoke in low tones.

His attire, from his dusty Hessians to black pantaloons and stylish jacket, bespoke quality without garishness. Mr. Rutland was no dandy or coxcomb.

Feeling Miss Sommerville's hostile gaze boring into her, Purity glanced in her direction and quirked a sardonic brow.

What had come over her to behave so insolently?

Had the nature she'd worked so hard to squelch these past years finally escaped?

"I don't know what you are about, Miss Mayfield." Miss Sommerville raked a critical gaze over Purity and found her wanting from the superior raising of her nose and eyebrows. "But you should know your place. Which I presume is that of a *servant*."

She hissed the last word as if she'd uttered a profane expletive or accidentally consumed an insect. A big beetle or a spider.

"A governess, to be precise." Purity fashioned a humorless smile and, in a wholly foreign fashion, let fly a verbal jab. "As, apparently, are you."

Purity Josephine Sapphira Shepard Mayfield, that is beneath you.

It was. Mrs. Shepherd would be horrified.

Purity felt rather gratified.

Spine gone rigid as a fire poker, Miss Sommerville jutted her dainty chin upward. Pure loathing shot from her eyes. "Why you..."

FIVE

I've accepted a new position as a companion to Mrs. Parmelia Templemore. My previous employer's sons objected to Mrs. Westcott gallivanting—their word, not mine—around the world once she reached her seventieth birthday. They insisted she move into the eldest son's home. She was quite broken-hearted at doing so and also to part ways with me. I felt the same. We'd grown close these past six years, as she has no daughter and I haven't a mother.

In any event, Mrs. Templemore and I shall attend the Earl and Countess of Mumford's house party, though we shan't arrive until Wednesday. Her ladyship is even more pious than Mrs. Shepherd and won't travel on Sunday.

As much as I enjoyed exploring the world, I am glad to be back in England. I hope to visit you, Joy, Purity, Mercy, Honoria, and Faith soon. I've missed all of you most dearly.

~Miss Trinity Ablethorne, in a letter
to Mrs. Chasity Terramier

. . .

Mottford Hall's Terrace
Several even more uncomfortable and awkward minutes later

As Theran left his aunt's side, he—and regrettably several other guests—caught the caustic exchange between Athena and Miss Mayfield. Well, to be perfectly fair, the overt hostility was entirely one-sided. Nonetheless, such exchanges should take place in private. To do otherwise always led to speculation and the spread of gossip by intrigued observers.

"I'll have you know that *my* father was a baronet. *I* am an aristocrat. A *lady.*" An unbecoming sneer contorted Athena's mouth as she scraped a contemptuous glance over Miss Mayfield. She eyed her as one might a warm cow patty upon one's gold-rimmed dinner plate.

Marcel Sommerville might've held a baronet's title, but by all accounts, the man had been a cockroach of a human being. A libertine who cared more about gambling, whoring, and his hounds than he did providing for his wife and daughter, he'd been set upon by padfoots as he left a gaming hell.

According to Imogene, he'd left his wife, Albertina, and Athena destitute.

Theran had never seen this side of Athena before—a side he was positive she contrived to keep hidden from him, but which didn't surprise as much as it ought to have done. Perhaps the fruit didn't fall far from the tree, given what he knew about her mother and father.

"Do you even know *who* your parents are?" Athena goaded with calculated and cutting cruelty. "Are you a by-blow born on the wrong side of the blanket and therefore must engage in employment?"

Athena was one to talk. She'd accepted her generous wages without hesitation each month.

Heads bobbed together as guests whispered to one another at the ugly exchange.

Aunt would not be pleased if she caught wind of the kerfuffle. Which she assuredly would. Nothing went on in Mottford Hall that Aunt Melvelia didn't eventually learn about.

Except for the slightest flaring of her nostrils, Miss Mayfield's composure didn't alter. Nor did she color as would most young women when flustered.

Theran had to credit her self-control.

Nevertheless, he'd bet his favorite horse Athena had hit a raw nerve. The signs were there if one looked closely. The abrupt shadowing of Miss Mayfield's brilliant green eyes. The contraction of the delicate line of her jaw. The squaring of her shoulders in an unconscious act of defense.

A queer feeling rooted around behind his ribcage—an inexplicable desire to protect her against Athena's uncharacteristic nastiness.

"Parentage does not assure gentility, a person's moral character, or basic decency," Miss Mayfield said in a perfectly pleasant tone. Eyes bright, she bowed her mouth a fraction. "As you have aptly demonstrated."

Touché.

Despite his disdain for public scenes, Theran couldn't help but agree with her witty assessment.

Pure loathing shot from Athena's eyes, and she half-raised her hand.

Blast and rot.

Elongating his strides, Theran hurried to close the distance between him and the women before an all-out row commenced on the terrace. A horrific image crowded his mind

—screeching women pulling each other's hair and their nails raking the other's face as enthralled guests looked on.

Aunt Melvelia would have an apoplexy.

"I would not, Athena," he said low and tense. "You are being observed."

She froze and cast a half-sullen, half-guilty glance toward him. Her cheeks ablaze with color, she curled her fingers into her palm, lowered her hand, and slid a covert peek around.

Several people had stopped to stare outright at the women. Theran forced his lips to curve into a congenial smile and stepped nearer, turning so that his back partially blocked the intrigued onlookers' view.

As for Miss Mayfield, she appeared coolly unaffected by the attention being directed their way and that she'd nearly been publicly slapped. Except...in the depths of her eyes, if he looked closely, anger and chagrin smoldered.

Dropping his attention, he took in her balled hands.

She'd wanted to slap Athena too. Or punch her.

The difference was, she hadn't given in to the urge and had conducted herself with admirable decorum. It made a person contemplate which woman was truly a lady and which was a hoyden. Or termagant.

"This person is impertinent beyond measure, Theran," Athena pouted. Voice lowered but shaking with outrage, she said, "She does not know her place and has insulted me. I demand she apologize and her employer be notified of her insolence."

In other words, Athena would have Miss Mayfield dismissed because she'd offended her.

Athena needed to grow thicker skin. People had a choice whether to become offended and fly into a dust. Besides, she was not without guilt. She'd tossed a few vicious verbal darts too.

He'd heard her.

Theran took Athena's elbow and pointed the fuming woman toward the house. "Athena, I require a word with Miss Mayfield in private. Why don't you take a few moments to compose yourself and perhaps even rest a short spell since Bernadine will be entertained for some time to come?"

A trickle of sweat slithered down his spine. Already warm, the day promised to become sweltering. He'd far rather be riding in his shirtsleeves, swimming in the pond at Atherley Hall, or enjoying the shade in the garden off his library.

Instead, he was reduced to arbitrating a spat between two grown women.

From the triumphant glint that entered Athena's eyes and the satisfied sideways glance she darted Miss Mayfield's way, she believed she'd won—that he intended to reprimand Miss Mayfield, or worse: inform her employer.

For some perverse reason, Theran didn't want to grant her that unmerited victory. Imogene had told him that Athena had a vengeful streak, and jealousy often influenced her behavior. In truth, he'd assumed she'd outgrown those childish tendencies long ago. Apparently, such was not the case.

He guided her a few steps away from Miss Mayfield. "Miss Mayfield wishes to speak to me regarding something she overheard when she found Bernadine."

Athena went still and noticeably paled. She swallowed and her brown eyes, unusually wide, blinked several times. Her focus swung to Miss Mayfield and then back to Theran.

Almost guiltily.

"Over...overheard?" The word emerged as a strangled croak.

Intuition fairly screamed a warning in his head. Eyes narrowed, he studied her. "Yes. In the secret garden."

He knew the garden well. As children, he and his older

cousins often played hide-and-seek there or caught frogs in the fountain. They'd even camped outdoors there on a few occasions.

During his aunt and uncle's annual house party, the private garden was also an escape from the activities and bustle. Few guests ventured so far from the house, and fewer still relished the isolation the garden provided.

Except, Miss Mayfield had. Else she'd not have found Bernadine.

Athena gave a little artificial laugh, which sounded similar to a bow torturing an untuned violin string.

"Surely you cannot trust *her*, Theran." Clutching at his sleeve, Athena said in a ferocious whisper, "She's a stranger, after all. And you heard how unpleasant she was to me. I would not put any faith in a word she says. Servants are notorious gossipmongers, spreading tattle hither and yon."

He dashed a glance toward Miss Mayfield, gratified that she appeared the epitome of indifference, even though she must've heard every unflattering word.

"Be that as it may, Athena, she has made the request, and as it concerns Bernadine, I shall hear her out."

Athena opened her mouth to argue, but Theran shook his head. "I'm not discussing it further with you. Go along, Athena. You appear quite overwrought, and I'm certain you do not wish to become the subject of chinwags. I believe I saw Lady Clutterbuck earlier, and I need not tell you what a chinwag she is."

Appearances meant everything to Athena—like mother, like daughter.

After another swift, antagonistic glare toward Miss Mayfield, studiously studying the flagstone pavers she stood upon, Athena gave a grudging nod. "All right, but I beg you not to be taken in by that creature. You know her not at all. Whereas you and I have been family for six years."

Theran merely inclined his head and then watched her disappear into the house. He had thought he knew Athena, and yet he'd learned more than one new thing about her this day.

Not flattering things either.

"Miss Mayfield. I've secured my aunt's salon for our conversation." He extended his arm to the door Athena had sailed through seconds before. "After you."

She veered her attention to the empty doorway then nodded.

"Of course, Mr. Rutland."

He fell in step beside her, their shoes echoing on the polished parquet floor. She looked neither right nor left at the landscape paintings gracing both sides of the passageway but kept her pert profile straight ahead. She was very well trained. They walked in silence until they arrived at the salon's entrance.

Theran opened the door and stepped aside for Miss Mayfield to enter.

The parlor reflected his aunt's eclectic taste, her preference for bold colors, and her enjoyment of gewgaws. Overstuffed armchairs covered in a floral brocade so gaudy they hurt the eyes to gaze upon sat at right angles to a sofa covered in the same unfortunate fabric. At least a dozen colorful, ruffled, and tasseled pillows occupied the seats. Gewgaws and whatnots smothered the doily-covered tables and shelves.

Miss Mayfield wandered to the center of the room and gazed about curiously—perhaps slightly aghast. The salon was quite a shock to the unprepared. The room reflected his aunt's innate vitality and unapologetic zest for life.

Several framed scriptures in neat needlepoint graced the

walls, and Aunt Melvelia's spectacles lay atop her well-worn Bible on the table beside her favorite seat on the sofa. A needle-point footstool of a cat sat before his aunt's preferred cushion.

After looking up and down the corridor, Theran paused for a second before shutting the door behind them. If Miss Mayfield had been a lady of quality, the door would've remained partially open. But as Theran didn't want anyone overhearing their discussion, and she was obviously in service, he'd chosen to shut the door.

It spoke to the perversity of the *ton* how no one fussed about the reputation of a servant, but an unchaperoned young woman of station could be considered compromised in the same circumstance. Another reason he had little use for *le beau monde*.

Arms folded, Theran leaned his shoulders against the panel and regarded Miss Mayfield through hooded eyes. He'd overheard her say she was a governess. Curious. Most governesses were long-toothed, long on the shelf, gravitated toward plumpness, and as plain as oatmeal porridge.

Purity Mayfield most definitely was none of those.

Where were her charges anyway?

Why wasn't she with them?

Cupping his nape with one hand, he said, "Tell me, Miss Mayfield. Are you in the habit of airing differences in public? I cannot imagine your employer approves."

SIX

I understand and respect your need for confidentiality and circumspection.

Regardless, I've been retained to investigate the disappearance of my employer's niece five and twenty years ago. He was told she died in a fire along with her parents, but evidence has emerged that indicates she may have survived the fire.

Recently found receipts indicate a history of payment to Haven House and Academy for the Enrichment of Young Women for many years by Lord Ballister. As I am sure you can imagine, the new Marquess of Ballister is keen to find his brother's child, if she is indeed alive.

As the child's legally appointed guardian, he had no knowledge of nor did he authorize the placement of his niece at your institution. He is hopeful this matter can be resolved without involving the authorities and without you being named an accomplice in this nefarious scheme.

~Jarman Embry, Esquire, in a letter
to Mrs. Hester Shepherd, proprietress of

Haven House and Academy for
the Enrichment of Young Women

The Countess of Mumford's Private Salon
A tension-filled minute later

Pretending to examine the salon's flamboyant decor, Purity counted to ten and then repeated the process.

A soft answer turneth away wrath.

A soft answer turneth away wrath.

Not this time.

When reciting the verse did nothing to dissipate her offense, she then recited a few more in her head. Mrs. Shepherd had insisted all of her pupils memorize scripture, and there was no shortage of verses Purity might call upon.

Be slow to anger.

Slow to anger calms a dispute.

Discretion makes a man slow to anger.

She would not react to Mr. Rutland's goading.

She. Would. Not.

Purity would simply tell him what she'd overheard, pray he was a sensible man and would protect his daughter, and be on her way.

Filling her lungs with air, she folded her hands together and brought her gaze to his.

Enigmatic deep-blue eyes regarded her, and she battled the urge to shiver and blush.

Sensible governesses did not flush crimson at the slightest provocation, nor did they take fright easily. Yet, Purity could not deny an air of animalistic power surrounded the man. It both appealed to her and made her cautious.

Compared to Mr. Rutland, Viscount Ceddes was slender, pale, and almost effeminate in his mannerisms.

A far, *far* different sort of man regarded her from across the room.

Purity felt rather like they were engaged in a verbal game of chess, though why Mr. Rutland felt the need to challenge her, she couldn't fathom.

"It is always preferable to have less than cordial discussions in private," she conceded with a slant of her head.

A rotted curl sprang loose and dangled near her cheek. She shoved the errant strand behind her ear and pretended not to notice the corners of Mr. Rutland's mouth twitching in amusement.

"But regrettably, as you witnessed, it is not always feasible."

Never mind that today was the first time she'd ever engaged in that manner of hostile discussion with anyone.

He levered upright, crossed to a table, and picked up a white porcelain cat figurine. It appeared small and fragile in his callused, sun-browned hand.

"You could've remained silent," he said, glancing over his shoulder. "Ignored Athena's comments."

Her cruel barbs and foul insults?

Naturally. Because Purity was a servant. She was expected to courteously accept whatever abuse was hurled her way.

Why did Mr. Rutland's attitude surprise Purity?

His ilk always favored bluebloods and aristocrats over the working class. They believed themselves superior in every way, even when their conduct spoke otherwise.

"I wonder, Mr. Rutland, would you have done so had your parentage been publicly disparaged?"

He lifted a shoulder and replaced the figurine amongst the others.

Purity pitied the maid assigned to dust this room. Every surface overflowed with knickknacks.

"As it has never happened, I cannot say." Hooking his thumbs together behind his back, Mr. Rutland faced her. "Are you?"

Taken aback, Purity gaped, unfamiliar heat rushing over her.

Was Mr. Rutland truly asking if she was illegitimate?

How crass and intrusive of the codpate.

He wanted the truth, then he could have it. Purity had nothing to hide nor be ashamed of.

If others judged her because of her parentage, there was nothing she could do about their ignorance or small-mindedness but hold her head up.

"I honestly do not know. I was raised in a foundling home."

Arrogant toad.

That was all she would say about the matter. It was none of his business.

"But if I were, Mr. Rutland, would what I wish to tell you be of less import?"

"No. You remind me of someone, is all. Though I cannot recall at this precise moment who."

He cocked a black eyebrow, his blue eyes penetrating in a manner that made her uncomfortable. Not afraid, but aware of him in a way she should not be.

"You are a governess?" He put a fingertip to another cat figurine—this one lying in a fur bed. "Yes? Where are your charges?"

Purity gave a cautious nod. "I am, for over eight years. I work for Viscount and Viscountess Ceddes. They collected their children for an outing this morning and aren't expected back until this afternoon."

So much for the coveted hours to herself.

An air of boredom emanating from him, Mr. Rutland folded his arms. His biceps bulged against the coat fabric. Given his bronze-skinned and muscular physique, Purity could not help but wonder if he was given to physical exercise.

She'd never witnessed Lord Ceddes exerting himself beyond lifting a wine glass or a cheroot.

"Now, what is it you wish to tell me?" Mr. Rutland asked, glancing at the French gilt-bronze and pink-marble mantel clock. "My daughter should return shortly, and I'm late for a cricket game."

Cricket?

Something very near disgust turned Purity's belly over. Such were the priorities of the elite. She didn't shy away from his direct gaze.

"I found Bernadine weeping inconsolably. I overheard Miss Sommerville berating her in the vilest way. She was unaware that I was in the hidden garden."

His raven eyebrows slashed together, and his well-molded mouth lashed downward.

"What, precisely, did she say?"

Purity gazed past him, concentrating on recalling exactly what Miss Sommerville had said. She was not a tattlemonger and would not embellish the telling.

"She called Bernadine a 'rotten little bratling. An ugly, miserable, motherless urchin who deserved to get lost.'"

With each word she uttered, Mr. Rutland's face grew tauter and more menacing.

He was, without a doubt, livid.

Pray God at Miss Sommerville and not her.

"Is that all?" The three syllables crackled with repressed outrage.

Purity suddenly wished it were all. Nevertheless, she bolstered her courage and forged onward.

"No."

Shaking her head, she suppressed an irritated groan when another tendril slipped free of its pin. If she were permitted to wear her hair with curls framing her face as was the fashion, she wouldn't regularly be re-pinning the stubborn things.

"Well?" Mr. Rutland prompted in a tone that lifted the hairs on the back of her neck straight up.

What was it about this man that set her senses on high alert?

Bracing herself for his wrath, Purity said in a breathless rush, "She called Bernadine a horrid little red-haired daughter of the devil."

Mr. Rutland said something beneath his breath that sounded very much like a vulgar oath.

He needed to know, but that didn't make the telling more agreeable.

"And Miss Sommerville said she'd lock Bernadine in her room again for three days with only bread and water to eat because she'd been disobedient and insolent."

At that, the angular planes of Mr. Rutland's face turned to granite. His eyes narrowed into flinty slits as he stared beyond her toward the window seat covered in an assortment of garish pillows.

This was a man one did not want as an enemy.

A man *she* did not want as an adversary.

Purity almost felt afraid on Miss Sommerville's behalf. Except, she didn't think Mr. Rutland was a violent man. He had every right to be furious at his daughter's treatment.

Unlike her friend Roxina Danforth, Purity wasn't the wagering sort. However, had she been inclined, she would've staked her savings that Miss Sommerville would not be remaining at Mottford Hall much longer. Or in the employ of Mr. Rutland either.

As it should be.

No person who treated a child with such contempt and cruelty should be permitted near them.

"Pray tell me," Mr. Rutland inquired with a derisive half-smile. "Why should I believe you, Miss Mayfield?"

SEVEN

I have told you before. I am not marrying some flibber-tigibbet with a fat dowry and prestigious lineage so that you can boast about your connections. I know my grandfather was an earl. I do not care. Evidently, you didn't either when you wed a commoner against his wishes.

I shall not be attending supper on the twenty-eighth of August so that you may introduce me to your hand-selected prospects. I shall be attending a house party.

I implore you, Mother, cease your meddling. You know Father would not have approved.

~Devin Everingham, in a note to
his interfering mother,
Mrs. Desdimona Everingham

An interminable five seconds later

Mr. Rutland's flagrant scorn ignited a spark of ire. Purity bit the inside of her cheek and forced a steadying breath into her lungs. There it was. The expected double standard. A person of Miss Sommerville's pedigree wasn't capable of despicable behavior, but because Purity was a servant, her word was in doubt?

"I do not lie, Mr. Rutland. In point of fact, your daughter told me that you say liars are the devil's mouthpiece. I am of the same opinion. Furthermore, my faith prohibits me from deceitfulness."

"*Faith*?" He gave a derisive snort. "What does your faith have to do with anything? For decades, I attended services weekly with hypocrites who professed one thing on Sunday mornings, but the rest of the week behaved as satan's own spawn."

Attended.

As in past tense.

"As have I. Nevertheless, amongst congregations, some are decent and upright every day. Those whose faith acts as a moral compass, if you will," Purity boldly countered. He had awakened a pugnacious tendency in her. "A person's breeding, station in life, or church attendance does not determine their character."

She'd just said something similar to Miss Sommerville.

"I'll thank you not to preach to me, Miss Mayfield," he snapped, those black eyebrows crashing together in displeasure. "Keep your pious, sanctimonious opinions to yourself."

Flabbergasted at his antagonism, Purity eyed him.

What had caused him to become so bitter?

The loss of his wife?

"If that is all..." The boorish lout gave the door a pointed glance.

Purity was half tempted to depart without telling him the

rest, but her conscience and concern for Bernadine would not permit her such selfishness.

"It is not."

His jaded appraisal pinned her to the wall.

"Of course it isn't," he drawled, pointing his gaze ceiling-ward. "You seem to have a penchant for carrying tales. Why am I not surprised that someone who affects such piety also has a propensity for gossip?"

"*Carrying tales? Gossip?*"

Purity nearly choked on her outrage. He was deliberately goading her. Poking the bear, as it were. And blast him to Hades, his tactic had worked.

Purity was good and truly incensed.

When was the last time she'd been this fuming mad?

Had she *ever* been this outraged?

Chin notched high, she glared daggers at him. "I take great care to only speak the truth. It is not my fault you are reluctant to hear it or that your blindness to your child's plight has put her in harm's way."

"Enough!"

The word uttered with lethal vehemence had the effect of a thunder bolt striking Purity.

Oh, she'd gone too far. *Much* too far.

A shiver of fear zipped up Purity's spine. Despite the heat of the salon, a tremor shook her.

"I beg your pardon," she said. "That was beyond the pale."

Purity wanted this discussion over. Now. She steeled her nerves. Blast her sense of righteousness and justice which demanded she tell Mr. Rutland everything.

"Whether you choose to believe me or not, you should also know that Bernadine had been slapped. A handprint was clearly visible on her cheek. She confided that Miss

Sommerville said that when she married you, she intended to send Bernadine to boarding school."

Purity checked the urge to retreat several paces at the murderous expression stamped upon Mr. Rutland's features. He'd balled his hands into fists, and for a heartbeat, she feared he meant to strike her.

After several more *tick-tocks* of the mantel clock, which matched the frenetic pounding of her heart, and the menacing rise and fall of his chest, his features relaxed into less intimidating, less feral lines.

"Thank you for telling me, Miss Mayfield." He pinched the bridge of his nose. "I appreciate your candidness. I shall have a discussion with Miss Sommerville to hear her side of the story and speak with Bernadine too. Naturally, I can rely upon your discretion regarding what you overheard."

Purity blinked rather owlishly.

Where had the rancor of moments before gone? He had reined in his black temper with apparent ease. Or practiced ability?

Purity wasn't sure whether the skill was admirable or disturbing.

Who was the real Theran Rutland?

Gentle, soft-spoken father or menacing blackguard?

"Of course, Mr. Rutland. As I told you, I do not gossip."

His nostrils flared as her arrow unerringly hit home as she'd intended it to.

He was commendable to insist on hearing all sides of the matter rather than jumping to conclusions or swift judgment. Still, given Miss Sommerville's past behavior, Purity expected the woman to lie without a qualm. And effortlessly smile the whole while.

Upon hearing a commotion in the corridor, Purity swung her attention to the door.

Thank God. She could escape this interrogation and this daunting man. For the remainder of the house party, she'd do her utmost to steer clear of him. She did not like verbal sparring.

"If you have no further need of me, Mr. Rutland, I shall excuse myself."

And perhaps salvage what remained of her free time.

The door swung open, and a startled Lady Mumford hovered in the entrance, her jaw slack. Miss Sommerville and three ladies Purity did not know peered over her shoulders, their expressions alive with conjecture and curiosity.

In point of fact, Miss Sommerville's was mainly smug.

"Oh, you *are* still here, Theran," the countess said to her nephew, on hand pressed to her throat in surprise. "Miss Sommerville assured me your meeting had ended. I see clearly that it is not."

She turned a dissatisfied glance to Miss Sommerville.

"I am terribly sorry, my lady. Please forgive me." Miss Sommerville ducked her head, chin to chest, in a theatric display of contriteness. "I must've mistaken one of the other menials for Miss Mayfield." *And pigs wear pink tutus and dance the ballet.* "They all look alike in their drab unflattering gowns and frumpy knotted hair, do they not? One would never mistake them, nor mutton dressed as lamb, would one?"

Two of the other ladies exchanged appalled glances, and Lady Mumford's eyes tightened the merest bit at the corners at the snide insult.

"I have never found it so," Lady Mumford said with just enough starch to reveal her disapproval.

Mr. Rutland caught Purity's eye, and she understood he knew Miss Sommerville was lying. The unspoken communication between him and Purity could not have been clearer if he'd said the words aloud. That they should be able to silently communicate, when only having just met, was as gratifying as it was bewildering.

Especially as but moments before, he'd challenged her honesty.

His handsome features had returned to the neutral expression the upper class affected so well. There was no evidence of the bitter man who'd discomfited her earlier.

He clasped his hands behind his back and rocked back onto his heels. "I apologize, Aunt. I shall require your salon for a few more moments. Miss Mayfield is just leaving, but I wish to speak with Athena."

His aunt's keen gaze shifted between him, Miss Sommerville, and Purity—lingering a disconcerting moment on her loose curls—before focusing on her nephew again.

She gave a brief nod and turned to her companions. "My dears, please make your way to the yellow salon. I'll be along in a trice. We must plan the theatrical performance for two Saturdays hence. It shall be the best yet, I promise you."

The women glided away, their heads together and no doubt speculating on the peculiar exchange in the salon. Purity had never before been the object of tongue-wagging, and it was not to her liking at all.

The countess took two steps away from the salon and then half-turned.

"Forsythia took Bernadine to the nursery, Theran. One of the maids I hired for the house party saw that she ate her midday meal and has tucked her into bed for a nap." She smiled, her kindly eyes twinkling. "She has decided that she must have a Dalmatian puppy for her birthday, Nephew, so prepare yourself."

"Thank you. I shall check on her shortly." Mr. Rutland's countenance spared no tenderness or sympathy for Miss Sommerville, who had become positively wan.

In truth, she looked rather sick, like she might cast up her accounts as she fidgeted with the pearls at her neck.

Running her fingers along the edge of her hand-painted fan, Lady Mumford shook her head. "I almost forgot. Miss Mayfield, the Ceddes returned moments ago. Lady Ceddes requires you to attend to the children at once. They are in the nursery."

They were early.

Had something happened?

Nodding, Purity made for the entrance. "I shall go up at once."

"There was an unpleasant incident with a goat, I believe," the Countess of Mumford said as she stepped aside for Purity to pass.

As Purity strode swiftly down the passageway—eager to put as much distance between herself and Mr. Rutland—his melodic baritone stretched into the hallway. "I no longer wish for you to act as Bernadine's governess."

The rest of what he said was muffled by hurried footsteps and the rustling of yards of fabric behind her.

"Miss Mayfield. Please wait a moment."

Purity stopped and turned around.

"My lady?"

Breathing heavily from rushing, Lady Mumford laid a beringed hand on Purity's forearm. "I do not know what you said to my nephew to cause him to dismiss that woman, but you have my profound thanks."

Of its own volition, Purity's attention gravitated to the almost closed door.

Somewhat startled at the vehemence of her hostess's declaration or that the countess would confide in a servant, Purity scrambled for an appropriate response.

"I but told him the truth, my lady."

Mr. Rutland would have to inform his aunt of the details if he wanted her to know them. Particularly after he'd all but called her a tattlemonger and liar.

"Well done, you." Beaming in approval, her ladyship patted Purity's arm. "I've always admired honesty. It is a true test of a person's character." She gave a sage nod, sending the feathers in her coiffeur bouncing. "The Lord detests lying lips, but he delights in those who tell the truth."

Purity smiled. "Proverbs twelve, I believe."

"Exactly so." Lady Mumford gave Purity an assessing look. "I should like to have a long chat with you during your stay, Miss Mayfield. Perhaps one day next week? After things have calmed a bit. The first week is always a frenzy."

Purity liked the Countess of Mumford. She was as genuine and kind a person as she'd ever met.

"Of course, my lady. If I can find time to leave my charges. This house party is a last hurrah, if you will, before they are off to school, so my duties are a bit uncertain."

"You leave that to me, my dear." A rather cunning smile wreathing her face, Lady Mumford bobbed her head again.

They parted ways, and Purity had the distinct impression she'd passed some sort of test.

Mulling over the emotional swings of the past several minutes, she hurried up the first floor and was about to ascend the next when Miss Sommerville made the first landing.

Gasping, she sputtered, "You...you...evil...conniving...lowborn...slattern."

With a hand on the banister and one foot on the first riser, Purity slowly pivoted.

Had Miss Sommerville run to catch up with her?

Her nose an unbecoming mottled red, tears streamed from Miss Sommerville's equally inflamed eyes. She raised a shaking finger and stabbed it toward Purity.

Purity planted both feet on the floor and braced herself for a verbal barrage.

"Theran was to have been *my* husband." Gown lifted to mid-calf, Miss Sommerville stomped forward, seemingly oblivious to the pair of women rounding the corner and stopping in their tracks. "We were neighbors for years. Then Mother married Poindexter Bambrick, and Theran met *Imogene*."

She spat the name with such malice a shiver scuttled across Purity's shoulders.

The ladies exchanged a disconcerted glance, apparently uncertain whether to proceed or retreat.

"Before he met my stepsister and she stole him from me, Theran was to have been *mine*!" Miss Sommerville practically ground her teeth in vexation. "I've waited years—*years*—and in a few minutes, you unrefined trollop, you've ruined everything."

Her voice rose to the ceiling in a demented shriek.

No, her deranged dream had ended when Mr. Rutland married her stepsister. Something, apparently, Miss Sommerville still raged over.

Turning cold glances upon Miss Sommerville, the ladies stood their ground.

Purity had the distinct impression that they did so to protect her.

"I did not threaten a child, Miss Sommerville, nor slap her in the face. You wish to blame me, but your actions alone have led you to this unfortunate juncture."

Purity was having a day of speaking her mind, it seemed.

Miss Sommerville took a menacing step nearer, her face contorted in such hatred that Purity took an involuntary step backward, coming up against the stairs.

"You shall pay, Purity Mayfield. I vow, if it is the last thing I do, I shall make you pay."

EIGHT

A visit to Trenthurst House is long overdue, Theran. I haven't seen Bernadine in nearly six months. I miss my only granddaughter. I'm not getting any younger, as you well know. We can celebrate her birthday as well as the birth of Jordan's third child.

Violetta's time grows near. Your brother would never admit it, but he's fraught with worry. Your presence would do him good. Raymond is at sea, but his last letter said he may return to England within the month. If so, I shall have my entire family together for the first time in two years.

Please do say you'll come, dearest. We miss you and darling Bernadine. Violetta has hired another nurse, so there is no need for you to bring Athena. You know Violetta cannot stand her.

Oh, and do give Melvelia and Herbert my love. I sent a note along with my regrets for missing this year's house party. I'm confident they understood that Violetta cannot travel due to her lying in, and naturally, I must be at her side.

~Mrs. Celena Rutland, in a letter
to her youngest son, Theran Rutland

Mottford Hall
Half-past eleven two evenings later

Theran released a tired sigh and plowed a hand through his hair as he trudged up the last few risers to the nursery level. He'd untied his neckcloth and unbuttoned his coat in preparation of retiring shortly.

At this hour, Bernadine would be fast asleep. Nevertheless, habits die hard. Every night that they'd slept under the same roof since Imogene's death, he'd kissed their daughter good night and told her how much her parents loved her.

Bernadine had no memories of her mother. She knew the beautiful red-haired lady wearing the golden gown in the portrait above the fireplace in the drawing room was her mama. Still, Bernadine had been an infant when Imogene had died.

Theran told her stories about Imogene and did his utmost to convey how much she'd loved Bernadine.

Was it enough?

Only two sconces burned in the shadowy corridor this time of night. Dozens of children's portraits—some a century old—hung from ruby cords above the wainscotting.

All was quiet in the way old houses were on their upper stories.

Two floors below, revelers yet enjoyed themselves with cards, games, spirits, and flirtations. A few of the more daring had secreted off for illicit rendezvous, which seemed inevitable at even the most virtuous of hosts' gatherings.

Last year, Aunt Melvelia had interrupted a couple *frolicking* on the rug before the fireplace in her private salon. She'd chased them half-clothed from the room, replaced the carpet, and scratched their names from her guest list.

"I cannot pretend ignorance of an offense I witness with my own eyes," she'd confided to Theran. "Not only were they copulating in broad daylight—can you imagine such blasphemy?—but both were married. And not to each other, mind you."

Aunt Melvelia had led a distinctly sheltered life, or perhaps her piety had protected her from the less savory aspects of society.

Theran wasn't convinced either was beneficial for women.

As he ascended the last riser, he permitted his mind to replay the unpleasant scene with Athena in Aunt Melvelia's salon. He'd had no doubt Miss Mayfield spoke the truth but had wanted to give Athena a chance to defend herself. It seemed fair, though what excuse she might conjure to justify her behavior, he couldn't fathom.

However, her stunt about his aunt's parlor being unoccupied not only established her deceptiveness, but it had also confirmed that it was grossly unwise to permit her any further care of Bernadine.

Still, he hadn't anticipated Athena throwing herself at him and declaring her unrequited love. How she'd waited in the shadows for years for him to notice her.

Uncomfortable didn't begin to describe his reaction to her protestations of devotion. He'd never thought of her other than as a sister—a cosseted, self-centered sister.

Athena had begged him to take her right there and then in his aunt's private salon. Her wrath when Theran had not returned her avowals but instead had firmly told her to depart Mottford Hall made him cringe inwardly again.

God's blood.

To think he'd entrusted his beloved daughter to the likes of Athena. Her conduct hinted at a mental imbalance. Once more, he kicked himself into next summer for being so blind.

When Theran had informed his aunt that he'd sent Athena on her way, Aunt Melvelia assured him plenty of extra maids had been retained for the party. He needn't fret about his daughter's care. Between the maids, his cousins who doted on Bernadine, and himself, they ought to manage for the duration of the house party.

Not an ideal arrangement, but it would suffice.

To Theran's knowledge, there'd been no issues thus far. His aunt had kept him so engaged with activities he'd had little chance to see Bernadine except for first thing in the morning and when he bid her goodnight.

Meanwhile, he would need to pen a letter to his man of affairs and set about finding a qualified governess, post-haste.

At once, an image of Miss Mayfield popped to mind.

No. Not a lovely young governess with marine-green eyes and satiny skin. He'd had his fill of young, pretty nursemaids with agendas, thank you very much.

A plump, matronly woman with frown lines and spectacles would suit. Maybe even a wiry hair or three upon her chin for good measure. One who didn't mind traveling because Theran was not leaving Bernadine again.

Where he went, his daughter went.

Yes, yes, such a person would do nicely indeed.

Decision made and feeling somewhat as if a burden had been lifted from his shoulders, he trod down the carpeted passageway until he reached the nursery. The door stood slightly ajar, and he toed it open.

Coals from a stoked fire sizzled in the hearth, and a turned-down oil lamp glowed atop the white and black marble mantel. Theran counted no less than eleven children fast asleep. A credit to their nursemaids and governesses, that.

Two more had arrived today, then.

An open door led to another chamber on the far wall where the nurses for the youngest children and the additional maids hired for the house party slept.

His aunt had informed him of those arrangements when he'd told her of his decision to dismiss Athena. Although, dismiss mightn't be the correct term. Theran had never exactly hired her.

She'd simply shown up on the Atherley Hall's doorstep one day, a carriage laden with trunks and luggage parked in the circular drive behind her. In typical Athena fashion, she'd announced she was there to act as Bernadine's nurse and governess. He still didn't know how she'd learned the prior nurse had married.

With Mottford Hall bursting to overflowing by week's end, governesses and ladies' companions shared the bedchambers lining the other side of the passageway—often four to a chamber.

Miss Mayfield sat on one of the beds, humming softly to a sleeping girl clutching a doll. It took him a moment to realize Miss Mayfield's hair covered her shoulders, and she wore a cloak over her nightdress. He could almost see her rushing to her charge's side, taking only enough time to snatch a cloak for modesty's sake.

Something unhitched in the region of his ribs.

This was a woman who truly cared for the children in her charge.

She bent and kissed the girl's forehead.

No, she loved them.

Something Athena couldn't even fake.

At his entrance, she glanced upward and put a forefinger

to her mouth, indicating he shouldn't speak. He swept his gaze around the long, rectangular room until he spotted Bernadine's little bed. She lay with one small fist above her head, mouth parted, and red hair spilling onto the pillow.

On silent feet, he wound his way through the other slumbering children to her bedside.

"Goodnight, my little rabbit," he whispered as he bent to kiss her warm, baby-sweet cheek. She didn't stir as he tucked the blankets more tightly around her small form.

How he loved this cherub—all that remained of his Imogene.

Three and twenty was far too young to die.

That truth didn't eviscerate him the way it had when his wife had first passed away. Now, rather than stabbing pain, it stirred a sense of melancholy—not only for himself but also for Bernadine. What she would never have.

No child should have to grow up without a parent—without her mama to guide her through the rites of becoming a woman.

Sensing someone behind him, Theran turned his head.

Miss Mayfield stood there, a cloud of hickory nut-brown hair about her shoulders and trailing down her back.

Didn't she plait her hair at night?

Or had her evening toilette been interrupted?

There was nothing the least bit alluring about the drab gray cloak covering her from neck to toes, yet something masculine and dormant stirred in Theran. With a start, he realized he not only found Miss Mayfield appealing, but he also desired her.

For the first time since his wife's sudden death, he felt attraction toward a woman.

Miss Purity Mayfield had rekindled his dormant passion.

The guilt he'd expected to follow such a revelation did not

bludgeon him. Instead, he felt more alive than he had in years. Three years, to be exact.

"Bernadine slept through Amaris's bad dream." With a tilt of her head, Miss Mayfield indicated the child she'd been comforting. She whispered, "A mama goat became upset when the children became too loud around her kids the other day. Poor Amaris was nearest the goat and received a head butt. The experience seems to have caused a nightmare tonight."

Ah, the incident with the goat Aunt Melvelia had mentioned.

"She's fine now, but I worry how she'll fare at boarding school next month when I am not there to soothe her. She'll have her sister of course, but..."

Her words trailed off as she caught her lower lip between neat white teeth. Averting her face, she blinked rapidly.

Was she trying not to cry?

"Am I to understand your time with the Ceddes children is nearly at an end?" Theran asked.

A wonderfully horrific, splendidly awful idea poked its knobby head up.

What about her?

Miss Mayfield would make a perfect governess.

He nearly threw his hands up to ward her off in the manner one would when encountering a demon or a witch.

No. No, by all of the saints, she would not.

Miss Mayfield was *not* rotund, wrinkled, nor did she wear spectacles. And no wiry hairs protruded from the velvety skin covering her slightly pointed chin. In short, Purity Mayfield was the opposite of what Theran wanted and needed in a new governess.

"Good night, Miss Mayfield."

If she was shocked at his abrupt dismissal, she gave no

indication. Any servant worth their salt learned to disguise their thoughts and feelings behind a benign facade.

"Good night, Mr. Rutland. I pray you sleep well."

"Don't," he snapped more harshly than he'd intended.

Eyes wide and pretty mouth parted, she blinked up at him. It was difficult to determine for certain in the muted half-light, but a hint of color appeared to tint the alabaster arc of her cheeks. "I beg your pardon?"

"Do not pray for me."

Theran sank onto the edge of Bernadine's bed, aware he was being an unmitigated arse and not giving a tinker's curse anyway.

"I stopped believing in God when He allowed my wife to die. If you want to believe in fanciful claptrap, that is your right. However, I'll thank you not to impose your nonsensical fairy tales upon me or my child."

With dogged determination, Theran turned his attention back to his daughter.

"I...Yes. Well. Good night then," came her soft contralto. "I meant no offense. Please forgive me."

Theran refused to look in her direction as she crossed to the door, her cloak making a soft *whoosh* as she moved.

Head bowed, he closed his eyes.

His reaction had been unfair, yet he could not regret setting Miss Mayfield straight. Except she hadn't actually said she'd pray *for him* to sleep well. Chagrin cascaded over him in castigating, searing waves.

Tomorrow, he'd apologize for behaving like a cad. He had no right to disparage her beliefs.

"Sleep well, little love." He kissed Bernadine's cheek again and after a final check around the room to assure himself all was well, made for the door.

"What are you doing?" Miss Mayfield's urgent, slightly

panicked whisper filtered through the door she'd left ajar. "You are intoxicated, my lord. Unhand me at once."

Theran threw the door wide.

A man he didn't recognize had Miss Mayfield pinned against the wall and was pawing her most brutally. Her cloak, a gray puddle, lay pooled on the floor around her feet. The rotter had torn the neckline of her night-rail and was planting wet, slobbering kisses on her throat and collarbone.

Her frightened gaze met Theran's across the span of the passageway. *Help me*, the almost black with terror orbs pleaded.

"Your tenure is ending as governess, Purity. But there's no reason we cannot come to a different arrangement," slurred the gentleman attired in the first stare of fashion as he continued to grope her. "I'm in search of a new mistress, and you will need employment soon. I can be generous when I'm pleased. And you please me very much indeed."

Lord Wendel Ceddes, Theran presumed. With invitees arriving over several days, he'd not met all of his aunt and uncle's house guests this year.

"You're drunk. Mad. I shall never be your mistress." Writhing and twisting, Miss Mayfield resisted his odious advances.

And yet, she did not scream.

Because she didn't want to awaken the peacefully slumbering children and servants? Or because she knew—astute woman that she was—that though she'd done nothing untoward, should others come upon her dishabille, she'd be thoroughly compromised?

Even a servant's reputation could be smudged beyond repair. Which was why so many women in service were obligated to submit to their employers' carnal demands. Acquiesce or be sacked, without a reference.

The world was an unfair, cruel place for women without means.

"Let me go," Miss Mayfield said through clenched teeth while trying to ward off Ceddes's advances.

She tried to box his ears, but he caught her hand in his and gave her a rough shake.

He chuckled, a deep evil rasp. "Didn't you wonder why you have a chamber to yourself? A few coins in a greedy palm works wonders."

Theran would be having a conversation with his aunt on the morrow. A dishonest servant could not be tolerated.

"I'd prefer you willing, Purity, but your disinclination shan't dissuade me. Surely after so many years in my employ, you know I get what I want."

"You...cannot...have me," Purity managed between gasps.

Fury sent Theran's blood to boiling.

This pizzle in a neckcloth would force her?

The bloody, rotten devil's spawn.

It had been a long time since Theran had used his fists on anyone. Not since he'd vowed to Imogene he'd never do so again.

But she was dead, and this reprobate needed to be taught an overdue lesson.

Theran stepped through the nursery door and closed it behind him.

"Let her go," he growled, low in his throat.

NINE

I find myself torn between honoring the confidentiality I vowed to keep and doing what is just and right in God's eyes. Your placement at Haven House and Academy for the Enrichment of Young Women was not the first time I'd contracted to accept a toddler. However, your benefactor misled me when he assured me no one wished to care for you.

You do, in fact, have an uncle. Paul Beckwith, the Marquess of Ballister, was named your guardian and only recently learned you survived the fire that killed your parents. Lord Ballister is most insistent that he meet you. I believe he is a good man—an honorable man, unlike his sire.

Toward that end, Purity, I have given him your direction at Petherwick Court. I anticipate this will be a shock for you, but in my heart, I know it is the right thing to do. You should never have been raised as an orphan. He intends to take you into his home and provide you the support that was due you. Whether you accept, of course, is a decision only you can make. Regardless, I hope you will pray for our Lord's guidance before you decide.

~Mrs. Hester Shepherd, proprietress of
Haven House and Academy for the
Enrichment of Young Women, in a letter
to Miss Purity Mayfield
- Forwarded to Mottford Hall

Still in the third-story corridor
An excruciating minute later

Mr. Rutland's fury-laden order disconcerted Lord Ceddes enough for Purity to wrest free of his unexpectedly strong grasp. Clutching her torn nightgown at her neck and bosom, she dashed several feet away. Her heart threatened to escape its confines, and her thoughts tumbled over one another as she cowered against the wall. Chest rapidly rising and falling and blood hammering a staccato in her ears, she sucked in air as her befuddled mind raced to assimilate her employer's attack upon her person.

God above.

The fiend had meant to ravish her.

In all of the years she'd been in his employ, his lordship had never hinted, in word or action, at his licentious nature. But then again, Purity typically encountered Viscount Ceddes only twice yearly. Usually for three or four days and always under the watchful eye of his attentive wife.

In hindsight, Purity understood that Lady Ceddes's attentiveness to her wayward spouse bespoke distrust rather than affection.

For a slight man, the viscount was far stronger than she'd have supposed. Her aching wrist gave testament to that fact. Purity had no doubt she'd sport a bruise as a result.

She shook her head to clear the hair clinging to her face—she dared not use her hands for fear of revealing herself to the men.

Face thunderous and appearing rather like an incensed bull intent on charging and impaling his lordship, Mr. Rutland had positioned himself into a pugilist's stance. His murderous glare would've given a wiser, less inebriated man pause.

Not so, Lord Ceddes.

The soused-to-his-immaculate-neckcloth jackanape was oblivious to the danger before him.

He curved his mouth into one of his practiced smiles, which his lordship no doubt presumed was disarming. It rather made him look reptilian—an uncharitable thought Purity had entertained on more than one occasion.

"I say, you'll have to wait your turn, my good man."

Viscount Ceddes squinted and gravitated his bleary-eyed focus between Mr. Rutland and Purity, his expression almost comical in his confusion. "Unless...you've already sampled her," he put in crudely. "Which explains why the chit is flitting about the corridor this late clad in her night-clothes."

His eyes shrinking to fury-filled slits, Mr. Rutland made a feral sound in his throat and advanced a menacing, predatory step. He appeared ready to throttle his lordship.

Despite Purity's fear and the shock making her shiver so hard her teeth chattered, gratitude filled her. In her entire life, no one had championed her before.

"And all this time, you've been pretending to be chaste as a nun, Purity." Lord Ceddes turned a jaundiced eye upon her.

"Had I known your true nature, I'd have taken advantage of your loose morals long ago."

A shudder of pure loathing scuttled up Purity's spine. She bit her tongue against the wholly unladylike retort demanding to be said. The man had all but implied she was a trollop.

"*Leave.*"

Shoulders hunched and expression feral, Mr. Rutland gritted out one clipped rage-induced syllable as if it took all of his self-possession not to pummel his lordship into next year.

Laughing, the viscount waggled a finger between Purity and Mr. Rutland.

"Not so fast, old chap." He swayed on his feet and hiccuped. "I want my turn."

Lord, he was good and pickled.

Purity wrinkled her nose. Even from here, she smelled the spirits wafting from him.

"I've waited a long time to sample this tempting morsel." His lordship gave a lewd wink.

The idiot still hadn't surmised Mr. Rutland wasn't a dissolute cohort in cahoots with him.

"My wife is worse than a Newgate warden, I tell you," Ceddes said. "Never permitting me five minutes alone with Miss Mayfield in eight years."

Well, that answered one question.

"The lady said no," Mr. Rutland bit out, the veins in his forehead clearly visible. "You will respect her wishes."

His restraint was admirable.

"*Lady?*" Ceddes scoffed, incredulous, before hooting with laughter. "Miss Mayfield is no lady. Would she work as a governess if she were?"

Though true, his blatant disparagement stung more than it ought to have done.

He regarded Purity, huddled against the wall. "In fact, she

is *still* in my employ. She'll do as I say, or she'll not receive a letter of reference." His gaze grew sly, and his lean jaw became taut. "I can make finding a new position very, *very* difficult for you, Purity."

An animalistic growl ripped from Mr. Rutland's throat. He snatched Lord Ceddes by the neckcloth and hauled him close, their noses practically touching. As Mr. Rutland was considerably taller, his lordship dangled there, the toes of his shoes scraping at the carpet.

"And I can make finding your teeth very, *very* difficult. Now leave, you whoremonger. I strongly suggest you and your family depart Mottford Hall first thing in the morning." Mr. Rutland spoke in a voice so cold and devoid of emotion that his words rivaled an arctic wind.

Purity shuddered and clutched her gown more tightly closed.

Rutland released his lordship so abruptly the man nearly fell onto his backside.

The viscount sputtered and choked but didn't quit the field just yet. "Who do you bloody think you are, ordering me about?"

A humorless grin arched Mr. Rutland's mouth.

"Theran Rutland."

Ceddes went chalk white, and beads of perspiration burst out upon his forehead and upper lips. The air left his lungs in a soft *whoosh* as if he'd been struck. He gave a stiff nod. "As you wish."

What did his lordship know about Mr. Rutland that would cause the arrogant toad to acquiesce with such alacrity?

Lord Ceddes raked a licentious gaze over Purity. He opened his mouth, but she blurted, "I quit."

She jerked her chin upward in proud defiance. She might

not have been born into a high station, but that didn't mean she would meekly tolerate abuse or disdain.

What was another couple of weeks anyway?

She could have her possessions forwarded to wherever she landed after this debacle.

Straightening his neckcloth, Ceddes gave a snide laugh. "Good luck finding a new position."

"She already has one as governess to my daughter at twice the wages, should she wish to accept," Mr. Rutland said.

Purity nearly choked on surprise at the casually uttered taradiddle. He needn't go that far to be rid of the viscount. Didn't he know the man would spread that tale about before he left? Then she and Mr. Rutland would find themselves embroiled in another muddle.

Better to tell the truth than try to extricate oneself from the web of deceit afterward.

"I'll just bet she does." Lord Ceddes' vulgar innuendo didn't go unnoticed.

Mr. Rutland's eyebrows crashed together as he towered over the smaller man.

"Should I hear a single whisper tarnishing Miss Mayfield's good name or reputation, I shall presume it originated with you, you mewling piece of human excrement." Each word was low and lethal. "You shan't like the consequences. Do I make myself perfectly clear?"

"Perfectly." With a superior sneer, his lordship took his leave, wobbling down the corridor before stumbling down the stairs.

Closing her eyes, Purity sagged against the wall. Her legs shook so mightily she wasn't positive she could remain upright much longer.

Mouth still dry from her earlier fright, she swallowed.

"Thank you, Mr. Rutland."

Why no one had come to investigate the commotion, she could not imagine. Probably because the entire vile encounter had been conducted in low tones and whispers. And because not all of the guests had arrived yet, some of the bedchambers remained unoccupied.

Purity sent up a silent prayer of thanks for small favors.

She felt the heat of Mr. Rutland's body and smelled his cologne before he gently asked, "Are you hurt?"

Only my pride and dignity.

She shook her head, and to her utter chagrin, a solitary, fat crystalline droplet trickled down her cheek. Mortified at the waterworks about to commence—Purity was not a weeper—she tucked her chin to her chest. Presenting her back, she surreptitiously wiped the corner of her eye with her bent forefinger as she rested her forehead against the wall.

Tears oozed from between her squeezed-shut eyelids, and her body trembled with the effort to suppress her sobs.

Mr. Rutland tenderly grasped her shoulders and turned her toward him. "Shh. Don't cry. It's all right. He's gone."

"I...I'm sorry." Purity swiped ineffectually at her wet cheeks, failing to stanch the salty flow of hot tears.

He made a distressed sound.

"I cannot stand to see a woman cry. Not even Bernadine." He gathered her into his arms, and Purity buried her face against the rugged wall of his chest.

At his tender touch, a sensation much like warm velvet enveloped her. Soothing yet sensual too, and wholly disturbing in its intensity. Despite her weeping, she breathed in his essence: sandalwood soap, starch, and his musky-woodsy cologne.

Clean and crisp—not heavy and cloying.

A fop Mr. Rutland was not.

At last, the reservoir of Purity's tears ran dry, and she lifted her head but kept her gaze averted. "Please forgive me. I've dampened your coat."

"No need to apologize, Purity." With his thumb and forefinger, he nudged her chin until she met his gaze.

His attention dropped to her mouth, and Purity had a sudden and wholly unexpected epiphany. He wanted to kiss her.

God help her. She wanted him to. Wanted to feel that firm mouth upon hers.

His head descended an inch, and she waited, breath hitched anticipation.

A neatly folded monogrammed handkerchief appeared beneath her nose.

"You were attacked and, in truth, handled yourself with estimable aplomb and bravery." His tenor had grown gruff as if he battled some inner force.

She blinked for a moment, chagrined and confused.

Had she misread him?

She'd not been kissed before, but every womanly instinct she possessed shouted he'd been a mere second from placing his lips upon hers.

"Thank you." Averting her gaze, she accepted the square. After indelicately blowing her nose and drying her face, she wadded the once-crisp cloth in the palm of one hand. She'd return the handkerchief after having it laundered.

"I am grateful for your intervention."

He gave her a cockeyed smile, and her tummy flopped over. It was her ragged nerves. Nothing more. It *couldn't* be anything more.

Bending, Mr. Rutland retrieved her cloak and extended it toward her with his gaze rooted to the carpet.

Only then did Purity realize her nightshift gaped open. A humiliated gasp hissed from between her teeth as she snatched the cloak and, with a practiced flick of her wrists, was shrouded in its comforting modesty.

"I should go." Filling her lungs with air, she met his sympathetic gaze. "Honestly, I'm surprised no one ventured into the corridor to see what the ruckus was about."

Head canted and his gaze somber, Mr. Rutland studied her.

The candles burning low in the sconces cast enigmatic shadows over the sharp planes of his face. Now that Lord Ceddes had taken his departure, Mr. Rutland appeared remarkably unruffled by the incident.

"What will you do?" he asked in the rumbling timbre Purity had heard for the first time today but would never forget her whole life long. Something about his voice resonated deep within her spirit.

"I'm not certain." She lifted a shoulder. She honestly didn't know, but that had been the case half an hour ago as well. The timeline had been expedited, was all, and she most assuredly had no character reference.

"I have some savings, and a friend has already invited me for an extended stay. I'll wait until the dust settles from this unfortunate affair before making a decision." She flicked her fingers back and forth to indicate the kerfuffle that had just occurred. "And I shall pray and seek the Lord's guidance."

In a blink, Mr. Rutland's features settled into granite lines, the sharp slash of his cheeks prominent in the dim light. His generous mouth turned downward in displeasure. Any mention of prayer or God and the man became frostier than the Highlands in January.

"I wish you well," he said stiffly before bowing and presenting his back.

Purity remained where she was until his footfalls faded down the stairs.

"I think I can safely presume there will be no forthcoming offer of employment."

Never mind at double the wages.

After making sure to lock her chamber door, Purity blew out the candle. Once settled upon the comfortable mattress with the counterpane pulled to her chin, she stared at the shadows dancing across the ceiling. Her earlier fright had dissipated, and one bothersome thought now plagued her.

How in the world would she explain Lord and Lady Ceddes leaving her behind like an old, discarded shoe?

TEN

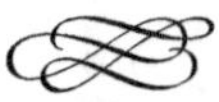

Please post a notice at the usual register offices and place adverts in several prominent news sheets.

I seek a mature woman, well beyond the typical age of marriage, to act as governess for Bernadine. Applicants must possess patience and a kindly temperament and be well qualified in academia, etiquette, and decorum instruction. Proficiency in French, drawing and painting, and musical talent are desirable. The competent candidate must be willing to travel frequently.

Time is of the essence. I should like to hire the new governess prior to visiting Trenthurst House in a bit over a fortnight.

~Theran Rutland, in a short missive
to his man of affairs, Severin Spottswood

Mottford Hall
Early the next morning

25 August 1818

Leaning back in the high back chair in his chamber, Theran reread the missive to his man of affairs. There was no time to lose in retaining a new governess. Last night, he'd decided to cut short his stay at his aunt and uncle's house party in favor of spending time with his immediate family at Trenthurst House.

Mother was right.

He should be with Jordan at this critical time, and he hadn't seen Raymond since Imogene's funeral. It would also be good for Bernadine to have time with her doting grandmother. Particularly after the ugliness with Athena. She'd left in high dudgeon within the hour of his dismissing her.

Good riddance to bad rubbish.

Theran blamed himself for the entire situation. He'd allowed guilt to override good sense, and his daughter had suffered the consequences for his poor judgment.

There was no help for it, however.

There would be whispers about Athena's departure. Quite likely about the Ceddes' hasty parting as well. And it wouldn't take much for an astute guest to determine Miss Mayfield was the common denominator.

As much as possible, he'd buffer his daughter, aunt, uncle, and cousins from the gossip. He wasn't certain he'd be able to do the same for Miss Mayfield, but Theran would try.

Satisfied the note would do, he sprinkled sand upon the damp ink. This morning, he must speak to his aunt and uncle about the Ceddes' departure and bring them abreast of the situation. As he shook the sand from the foolscap, Purity Mayfield's image intruded upon his thoughts.

Last night, she'd exemplified courage and composure, and Theran couldn't help but admire her fortitude. Yes, she'd wept, but only after the unpleasantness was over and shock had set in.

What woman wouldn't have done?

He purposely put from his mind the blurted offer of employment. The hasty declaration had been a means to an end. To be rid of Ceddes and to assure Purity's safety.

Theran hadn't been serious—he couldn't be.

The tantalizing image of the creamy skin exposed by her ripped gown flashed to the forefront of his mind. *No, fiend seize it.* He would not entertain such thoughts about the pretty, vivacious governess.

Theran could not hire her.

To do so would be the height of folly. He pinched the bridge of his nose and shook his head, reaffirming to himself he'd made the right decision. It would take a ruling in the House of Lords to persuade him otherwise.

Not only was Purity Mayfield the opposite in physical appearance of what he deemed an ideal candidate, but she was too young and far too religious for his taste. She'd likely insist on saying grace at meals, praying before bed, and attending services every Sunday.

He'd spare Bernadine the heartache of unanswered prayers and dashed hopes by sheltering her from such nonsensical rot.

You believed at one time.

Yes, before his prayers, which had turned into pleading— then begging and bargaining— for Imogene's recovery, went unanswered.

He pushed the intrusive thought to a fusty recess in his mind.

Folding the foolscap, Theran glanced to the door and then the miniature brass-cased carriage clock on the nightstand.

A quarter past eight.

It was still early, but normally, Bernadine greeted him first thing upon awakening. Perhaps no maid had been available to escort his daughter to his chamber this morning.

Once he'd sealed the letter, he tucked it into his jacket pocket.

First, Theran would seek his aunt and uncle and apprise them of the situation with the Ceddes and Purity, then wish his daughter good morning. Hopefully, Spottswood would promptly find suitable candidates for a governess, and Theran could conduct interviews next week at Mottford Hall. Mayhap his aunt would be willing to sit in on the discussions.

Satisfied with the course he'd selected, Theran left his chamber.

He passed the letter to a footman in the foyer a few minutes later. "Would you see that this is posted at once, Dowell?"

Theran handed the fellow a few coins, including a generous tip.

"At once, Mr. Rutland." Grinning, Dowell put two gloved fingers to his forehead.

Somewhere in the house, a clock chimed the half-hour. His aunt would be in her salon attending to her morning devotions.

Every day, without fail, from eight to half-past.

Good God.

Was that something Miss Mayfield did as well?

Yes, indeed. It was wise to have kicked the preposterous notion of hiring Purity to Timbuctoo. Never again would he permit his mind to trudge down the rocky track.

"I say, Rutland," Devin Everingham called. "You stood us up for the cricket match. We lost, and Grafton has had a jolly good time rubbing our noses in it for the past two days."

Theran faced the stately curved staircase.

Everingham, accompanied by Hemsworth, sauntered

down the dark walnut steps. Both appeared a bit bleary-eyed. Likely, they stayed up far too late and drank far too much. Before he met Imogene, Theran would've been right there with them. Now such pursuits didn't appeal.

"Are you on for the boat race today, or do we need to find a third?" Hemsworth asked before yawning widely.

"Forgive me." Theran offered an apologetic grin. "An urgent incident with my daughter required my attention. Nothing else would've kept me away."

He hadn't had a chance to talk with either and apologize. If there were fewer than a hundred people here already, he'd have been surprised.

"S'pose you're forgiven then," Everingham allowed. He did a sweep of the entry before saying, "Bernadine is well?"

Theran nodded. "She is."

"Heard there was a bit of a dustup with Miss Sommerville the other day," Hemsworth ventured.

Of course they'd heard. Undoubtedly, so had the rest of the guests.

"Yes." Theran gave a curt nod. He'd prefer not to discuss the details when anyone might come upon them. "She has returned to her mother's home."

Her stepfather's too, but Athena had never taken to her mother's second husband.

"Prudent on your part." Hemsworth nodded and brushed his chin with his hand. "Never liked the chit. She always looked at you like a sweetmeat she wanted to devour."

"You might've told me that before. I only just became aware of Athena's tendre," Theran said, unable to completely hide his derision.

"Nothing for it." Offering an apologetic grin, Hemsworth held up both hands. "I don't poke my nose in others' business."

"Since when?" Everingham guffawed. "You love nothing better than to offer unsolicited advice."

"Stow it, Everingham," Hemsworth grumbled good-naturedly.

For all of their bantering, they were the best of chums. Loyal and trustworthy fellows, and Theran counted himself fortunate that they were amongst his friends.

"Ah, there you are, Theran." Uncle Herbert, wearing his usual charcoal-gray suit and immaculate cravat, his mouth curved into his perpetual smile, strode into the foyer. "Your aunt and I would like a word with you before breakfast, please."

What now?

ELEVEN

Permit me to introduce myself. I am Paul Beckwith, Marquess of Ballister, your paternal uncle. Your father, Clarence, was my younger brother. I have only recently learned that you did not perish in the fire that took your parents' lives. Your father and mother named me your guardian, and had I known you lived, I would've taken you into my home and raised you with my children.

My wife, Ellise, and I should like to invite you to make our home yours. We understand that at eight and twenty, you've made a life for yourself. At the very least, please do come for a visit and meet your cousins, Uncle Toliver, and Aunt Therese. We all wish to know you.

Your given name was Caroline Aimee Beckwith, if you wished to know.

~Paul Beckwith, Marquess of Ballister,
in a letter to his long-lost niece,
Purity Mayfield (Caroline Beckwith.)
Posted to Petherwick Court and burned
by Viscount Ceddes after reading

. . .

Servants' Quarters—Mottford Hall
Early Morning
25 August 1818

Having given up on sleep well before dawn, by six of the clock, Purity had packed, dressed, and deliberated whether to venture to the nursey to bid Pomeroy, Merrilee, and Amaris a farewell. In the end, dread of encountering either Ceddes parent, resulting in an unpleasant ruckus and upsetting the children, had rooted her feet to her room.

For the first time in her life, Purity had chosen the coward's way, and she didn't at all like how she felt afterward. She'd prided herself on her courage and resilience. It didn't matter that she'd done what was best for the Bardslay children.

Merrilee, Amaris, and Pomeroy wouldn't understand why, after eight years, Purity wasn't going with them. Or, for that matter, why they were leaving just a day after arriving at the Mumfords' when their parents had actually spent time in their company yesterday. Nonetheless, with his gift for lying, Lord Ceddes had likely concocted a credible story.

Perhaps Lady Ceddes, fully aware of her husband's foul penchants and resigned to the consequences, hadn't needed an explanation. *Poor woman.* She might possess fancy clothing and jewels, opulent estates and houses, wealth, status and position, and have servants at her beck and call, but she lived with her husband's perfidy every single day.

If Purity lived to be a hunched over, wizened, one-hundred-year-old crone, she'd never understand marriages of convenience or arranged marriages. Why exchange vows if one didn't intend to honor them? If one fully intended to take lovers and engage in infidelity, regularly and nonchalantly?

For the first time in a long while, she considered her parents.

Who were they?

What circumstances had caused her to be discarded and sent to live at Haven House and Academy for the Enrichment of Young Women? Someone had paid the substantial monthly fee, which suggested at least one of her parents came from a family of influence.

Ah, well. There was naught Purity could do about that. Her energy was better spent focusing on her future and not the past.

Wrapping her arms around her shoulders, more for comfort than against a chill, she shook her head. The thick beige, plum, and leaf green flowered Aubusson carpet she paced across muffled her footsteps.

How soon before she could ask for a coach to take her to London?

Would the Mumfords object to the inconvenience?

She didn't think the countess would. The earl might, however.

Purity's gaze fell on the small, neatly made bed, her worn unassuming satchel on the floor beside it. Two more beds with matching counterpanes occupied the same wall. Here she'd believed her lack of roommates was because all of the guests had not yet arrived, when in fact, Lord Ceddes had bribed a servant to make it so.

She smoothed her hands down the front of her dove-gray gown, accented by charcoal braid and ribbons. It wasn't a traveling gown, but how many governesses could claim to own one?

Her wardrobe consisted of exactly seven day gowns, one mourning gown, an old, drab affair she used to conduct outdoor activities, and a single pretty maroon gown for more formal affairs.

How Purity would get the rest of her possessions from Petherwick Court, including the silver cross Hester Shepherd had given her when she left Haven House and Academy for Young Women, she simply didn't know. She wouldn't be shocked if Lord Ceddes burnt them out of spite.

Mayhap she could impose upon Lady Mumford or Mr. Rutland to request them on her behalf. Lord Ceddes had been afraid of Mr. Rutland. That had been obvious.

Mr. Rutland's features, the rakish tilt of his lips, and ebony eyebrow arched in an eloquent fashion promptly invaded her musings. He'd been a godsend last night, saving her from almost certain despoilment.

He'd almost kissed her.

She'd wanted him to.

What kind of depraved woman did that make her?

Biting the nail of her forefinger and hidden in the fern-toned draperies, Purity stood to the side of the window. Unlike many aristocrats, the Mumfords had spared no expense for the servants' chambers. They were as well furnished and comfortable as any guests', which spoke to her hosts' generous and magnanimous nature.

The Ceddes' coach had arrived before the grand entrance some fifteen minutes ago. Footmen loaded the luggage with practiced efficiency.

Tears threatened, but Purity summoned every ounce of stalwartness and blinked them away. As her vision cleared, the sleepy-eyed Ceddes family emerged from the house. This was the earliest Purity had ever seen his lordship or her ladyship out of bed. Their pinched, peevish expressions conveyed their displeasure at the inconvenience.

Dressed as a miniature gentleman and his chin tucked to

his chest, Pomeroy held his sisters' small hands. He attempted to hide his sorrow, but the girls openly wept.

Purity's heart wrenched, and she bit her lower lip to temper the cry hurtling to her throat.

Unfair. Unfair, her soul wailed.

It wasn't those sweet innocents' fault. Regardless, they suffered for their father's sins. God curse Lord Ceddes for a reprobate and libertine. A neglectful and self-centered father, an adulterous degenerate, and a pinch-penny, demanding employer.

Amaris lifted a tearful face toward the upper windows as if she searched for Purity.

Purity couldn't resist waving and was gratified to see a small smile curve Amaris's mouth. She said something to her siblings, and they all three peered upward.

Purity moved into full view—devil take Lord Ceddes—and blew them a kiss. They must not depart thinking she didn't love them.

A soft scratching came upon her bedchamber door.

"A moment, please." She raised her gaze ceiling-ward and whispered a quick prayer of favor and grace that it wasn't a note asking her to depart the premises post-haste.

With a final, heartrending glance out the window, Purity gave one last wave. The children waved but stopped abruptly when their father snapped something and swung his attention upward.

Heart hammering in her chest, Purity retreated into the draperies' protective shadows.

A knock sounded again.

She forced herself to cross the chamber on wooden legs, unlock the door, and with composure she was far from feeling, accept the neat rectangle from the fresh-faced maid.

Too much to hope it was a letter of reference after all.

"Thank you," she told the wide-eyed maid whose gaze lingered a fraction on the packed satchel before darting away.

"I was told to wait for a response, Miss."

That was odd.

Forehead furrowed, Purity opened the folded sheet, and grateful tears sprang to her eyes.

I am uncertain what has prompted your employer's hasty departure, Miss Mayfield. Nonetheless, I would be ever so grateful if you could remain for the duration of the house party as Bernadine's governess. I shall pay you generously for the inconvenience.

M. Mumford

WHAT INCONVENIENCE?

Lady Mumford had provided an unexpected blessing.

Purity wasted no time in penning a brief affirmative response. Nearly a month more employment and wages before she had to impose upon Chasity was a welcome reprieve. How the Countess of Mumford had convinced her nephew to agree, Purity wasn't sure. Despite the circumstances, she quite looked forward to getting to know Bernadine.

ENTERING THE NURSERY A FEW MINUTES LATER, Purity steeled her resolve and summoned a sunny smile for the other servants. Undisguised surprise and curious stares met her entrance—a few exchanged startled glances as well.

"Good morning." Her face might crack from the artificial smile. "At Lady Mumford's request, I shall be acting as Miss Bernadine's governess for the duration of the house party."

Still in her nightgown, Bernadine squealed in delight and launched herself at Purity. "I'm so happy!"

Laughing, Purity lifted the little girl. "Let's get you dressed, shall we?"

"Can we see the puppies this morning?" Bernadine asked as she wiggled out of her night gown behind a strategically placed screen. In the process of pulling a stocking on, she implored, "Pl-*ee*-ase, Purty?"

"You must call me Miss Mayfield now, Miss Bernadine," Purity gently instructed as she lowered a pretty ruffled pink gown over the child's vibrant curls.

Bernadine titled her head, her green eyes bright with intelligence. "Cause you're my governess now?"

"Yes, dear."

Dutifully presenting her back for Purity to fasten her frock, Bernadine mumbled, "Grown-up rules are silly."

Yes. Yes, they often were.

"You didn't answer me 'bout the daldamayshins," Bernadine said, sliding her little feet into her shoes.

Purity couldn't help but smile as she led Bernadine behind the screen. "Yes, you may see the puppies after breakfast."

"I want to see puppies too," declared a handsome little chap with a shock of red hair even brighter than Bernadine's gingery locks.

"Me too," and "I want to see them," echoed throughout the nursery.

Purity held up a staying hand.

"Everyone must get dressed and eat breakfast first. Then, if your nursemaids and governesses agree, we can have an outing to the stables to visit the puppies. But only if you promise to be very quiet and well behaved. We don't want to scare the babies or upset their mama, do we?"

Little heads with earnest gazes shook back and forth.

Hopefully, Purity wasn't overstepping the bounds by agreeing to take the children to the stables without seeking permission first.

"Come on then." A cheerful maid with an Irish accent herded two tow-headed chaps toward their beds. "The sooner you are dressed and have eaten, the sooner we can be off to the stables."

Purity hoped they wouldn't encounter Mr. Rutland. Though grateful for his intervention last night, he was the most irreverent man she'd ever encountered, and he stirred things in her that were better left dormant. She needed to get a firm grip on her riotous emotions before facing him again.

TWELVE

Ronan Brockman suggested if you have the room, plant corn and potatoes as they are consumable by humans and livestock. True, they are not as popular here as in America, but that might give you an edge on the market.

Forgive me for the curtness and shortness of this missive.

I foolishly hired a female scrivener after losing a bet. Faith Roth is determined to make my life purgatory. I confess she is a capable amanuensis but does not know how to keep her opinions and suggestions to herself. I've never been tempted to muzzle a female before, but so help me, God, I may invent a sticky ribbon of some sort that permits me to temporarily seal her mouth shut.

~Constantine, Lord Kellinggrave, in a note
to his friend, Theran Rutland

Still in Mottford Hall's foyer

"I'll meet you at the lake at half-past ten." With a wave to his friends, Theran fell in step with his uncle.

"Heard there was a bit more dramatics last night, my boy."

Quirking an eyebrow, Theran met his uncle's merry gaze. "I suppose that's one way to put it."

"House parties never used to be so complicated." Pulling his ear, Uncle Herbert made a sound in his throat. "Melvelia adores hosting, though. Cannot deny her the enjoyment."

Because Aunt Melvelia had a generous nature and a big heart.

Their boots clacked in unison as they walked the remainder of the way in companionable silence. A few moments later, they entered Aunt Melvelia's private salon.

Glancing up, she curved her mouth into a welcoming smile and removed her spectacles.

"I see you found him, my dear."

Married nearly thirty years, his aunt and uncle's adoration for one another bordered on embarrassing. Childless for the first ten years, they'd given up having offspring. Then his three cousins had come in rapid succession. Aunt Melvelia vowed the Lord had opened her womb like Sara, Ana, and Rachel in the Bible and freely told the tale to anyone who would listen.

"You wished to speak with me?" Theran gave her an affectionate peck on the cheek she angled upward. "I haven't bid Bernadine good morning yet, so though I do not wish to rush you, I'd prefer not to tarry long."

His aunt laid her Bible and spectacles aside. She gave a little wave in the air. "La, no need to fret over the dear. I've asked Miss Mayfield to attend Bernadine."

His aunt's temerity brought Theran up short. He gave his beaming aunt a cautious look.

"You have?"

Seemingly oblivious to Theran's less than cordial response,

she nodded. The feathers atop her turban bobbed with the movement. Today she rather reminded him of a peacock in her colorful gown of royal blue, green, and teal. In his staid, unadorned suit, Uncle Herbert more closely resembled a blackbird.

They gave credence to the adage that opposites attract.

"Indeed. I did," Aunt Melvelia agreed with an enthusiastic nod. "The moment I learned early this morning that the Ceddes were leaving, I sent a note to Miss Mayfield asking her to stay on and attend Bernadine for the duration of the house party. She has graciously agreed."

Theran stifled a groan.

Just perfect.

His aunt clapped her hands as if she'd come upon the most brilliant of solutions. "It's perfect, is it not? You require a governess and Miss Mayfield needs a position."

"No, I fear, I do not." Theran shook his head. "I posted a letter to my man of business a few minutes ago asking him to place adverts for a governess. Regrettably, Miss Mayfield will not suit."

"I am most disappointed to hear that, Theran. I quite like Miss Mayfield." His aunt's face fell, and she sent her husband an imploring look. "I wonder what she will do?"

At once, Uncle Herbert crossed to her and took her hand.

"My boy, we don't mean to interfere, but perhaps you have insight into the Ceddes' premature departure?" Uncle Herbert kissed his wife's fingers and gave her a tender smile.

To be that much in love after so many years...

Something twisted behind Theran's ribs.

It took him a heartbeat to recognize the emotion as envy.

He would never have what they had.

"They were rather closed-mouth about their reason," Uncle said, resting a hand upon Aunt Melvelia's shoulder.

I'll bet they were.

Lady Ceddes had probably been fed a cock and bull story by her coxcomb of a husband. Theran would've liked to have been an invisible observer during that conversation. Ceddes explaining the hasty parting and leaving Miss Mayfield behind would've taken ingenuity. Although, Lady Ceddes would have to be blind and deaf to be unaware of her husband's adulterous propensities.

Rubbing his jaw, Theran sighed and wandered to the mullioned window.

As he passed her, Aunt Melvelia's Persian cat, Precious Puss, curled atop a pink tasseled cushion, cracked a blue eye open. After giving Theran a condescending glance, she went back to sleep.

A cloudless azure August sky met his perusal through the spotless window. A perfect day for the boat race and picnic afterward. He quite hoped for Scotch eggs. Already, servants scurried about erecting tents and placing tables and chairs on the plush green carpet.

Bernadine would adore both activities.

Wisest to be straightforward with his aunt and uncle about last night without going into the distasteful details. He tossed a glance over his shoulder, unsurprised to see both staring at him with patient, yet expectant, expressions before returning his attention to the grounds.

He'd far prefer to be outdoors than having this troublesome conversation.

A few intrepid guests strolled the lawns and gardens. A shiny red head caught his attention. Bernadine held Miss Mayfield's hand as she, three other adults, and a half dozen or so children descended the terrace steps.

He didn't need to be told where they were going—to see the puppies.

That reminded him.

He needed to find out which pup Bernadine favored. A puppy would make an ideal birthday gift and provide her with companionship. His uncle would be delighted to permit Bernadine her pick.

If Theran made haste, perhaps he could catch them and see which puppy his daughter preferred.

"Miss Mayfield was set upon by Ceddes outside the nursery last evening. His motives were not honorable." Clasping his hands behind his back, Theran faced his aunt and uncle. "Had I not been in the nursery bidding Bernadine good night and able to intervene on Miss Mayfield's behalf, she would've been...*ruined*."

Theran could not bring himself to say *raped* to his aunt.

She'd probably faint dead away.

"Never say so!" A scowl furrowed Uncle Herbert's usual placid forehead. "The rotter dared such scandalous behavior in my home?"

Her face ashen, Aunt Melvelia pressed a hand to her ample chest and gasped, "He did not!"

"He did." Theran grimaced, renewed outrage heating his blood as he recalled the ugly incident. "I'll spare you the sordid details, but it was most unpleasant. Miss Mayfield emerged, if not completely unscathed, at least uncompromised. I advised Ceddes it would be in his best interest to depart this morning with his family."

"Well," huffed Theran's aunt. "I shall see that doors are closed to the bounder." Her plump face creased in concern. "And you're certain Miss Mayfield is all right? She made no mention of the incident in her response to my note."

Not a surprise.

Servants did not complain to their employers if they

wished to keep their positions. And a female servant would not disclose such an interlude for the same reason.

Leave it to his kind aunt to fret over a servant. But then, she treated everyone as equals. More people ought to.

Theran considered her question. "I believe so. Miss Mayfield possesses remarkable fortitude."

Intelligence, kindness, and integrity as well. All admirable qualities in a governess.

No.

She was too young and too religious.

You don't know if she's religious. That's just an excuse, and you know it.

Of its own volition, his attention strayed to the windows. The small entourage made slow progress. Every few feet, a child stopped to inspect an insect, a flower, the geese flying overhead... Or one of the adults brought their attention to something or other of interest.

Never let a possible lesson pass.

"Don't fret, my dear." Uncle Herbert patted his wife's hand. "You have such a good heart. You can still provide Miss Mayfield with a letter of reference for her time at Mottford Hall."

"Why, yes, I can." Aunt Melvelia brightened considerably. "What a brilliant notion, Herbert. I shall do that very thing."

Unaccountable relief eased the tension knotting Theran's shoulders he hadn't realized was there. Had he been unconsciously concerned about Miss Mayfield's future prospects?

No, he'd been aware her situation was precarious, but she'd claimed to have funds and somewhere to go.

How long would either last?

Why was he worried about it?

In truth, as appalling as last night's episode had been, at

least Theran had been there to protect Purity. Had she been at home...well, the thought didn't bear completing.

That reminded him.

"You should know, Ceddes said he bribed a servant to ensure Miss Mayfield had a chamber to herself."

"By thunder," exploded Uncle Herbert in an uncharacteristic show of anger. "I shan't have such underhanded shenanigans in my home."

Uncle Herbert did not curse in front of his wife.

"I shall get to the bottom of this today, I tell you," he vowed.

"Question the new upstairs maid. I trust our regular servants," Aunt Melvelia said, her brow stamped with worry.

A pinched expression had replaced her earlier joy. "By the by, Theran, Lady Clutterbuck and Mrs. Armitage overheard Athena threatening Miss Mayfield before she left. They were quite concerned at the vehemence Athena demonstrated. She has vowed to get even."

THIRTEEN

Expect us no later than the tenth of September. I don't wish to offend Aunt Melvelia or Uncle Herbert by leaving too soon. They've gone to great effort to be accommodating. I am seeking a new governess for Bernadine, so you needn't fret about Athena. Please give Violetta and Jordan my warmest regards.

~Theran Rutland, in a letter
to his mother, Mrs. Celena Rutland

Path to Mottford Hall Stables
An hour later

Deliberately keeping her attention focused on the red-haired cherub whose hand she held, Purity led the way along the well-trod path.

No one questioned why she remained at Mottford Hall when her employers had left, and Purity didn't volunteer a reason. Nevertheless, she didn't like being the object of speculation. It felt rather like being undressed, laid bare without permission for others to gawk at.

Two nursemaids and governesses tromped behind her with a total of eight very excited children. The rest had opted to stay behind with the youngest children.

Bernadine tugged at her hand. "Miss Mayfield?"

"Hmm?" Purity brought her meandering thoughts back to the present. "Yes, Bernadine?"

Hop. Hop. Hoppity-hop.

With the pride of one who'd already seen the pups, Bernadine said, "The puppies are all white."

"Indeed?"

"Uh-hum." Tongue poking from the corner of her mouth, Bernadine stared at the gravel path before her. *Hop. Hop. Hop.* "Cousin said the babies get their black spots later."

"I didn't know that." Purity had never been around dogs.

"Do you think Papa will let me have a puppy?"

Hop. Hop.

Bernadine hopped over a stick, sending her ringlets to twirling.

"I cannot say, I'm afraid."

Purity would not give the child false hope. However, her father doted on her, so the idea wasn't farfetched.

They were nearly upon the large barn. A stable boy of perhaps twelve years old gave them a toothy smile as he loped inside the wide-open doors. Two more stable hands led a pair of majestic horses from the building to a corral several feet away.

With a white mane and tail, the roan must be at least

fifteen hands tall. The gelding's muscles rippled beneath his glistening ginger-tinted coat.

Bernadine pointed. "That's my papa's horse."

"He's magnificent."

Rather like his master.

Purity nearly stumbled at the intrusive thought. Other than his kindness last night, Mr. Rutland had been a boorish clod to her.

Don't forget the almost kiss.

"What is his name?" Purity asked, still shaken at her wayward musing.

"White Flame."

"What a perfect name."

A gentle breeze teased her straw bonnet's white ribbons. She'd opted not to wear her spencer. Even her gown felt a bit cloying already, and the day was young.

"I helped Papa name him," Bernadine said proudly. "He's orange like a fire. But his tail and mane are white. Fire can be white sometimes."

"What a clever, creative little girl!"

A smile of pure joy blossomed across Bernadine's face.

She gestured for Purity to bend near. Upon doing so, the child threw her arms around Purity's neck and hugged her fiercely.

"I hope my papa marries you."

Oh dear.

Fearful the other adults had earwigged on the whispered declaration, Purity glanced up and froze.

Oh, my God.

Her lungs ceased to function, and she struggled in vain to draw a breath.

There stood Theran Rutland, and from the darkening of

his inscrutable gaze to midnight blue and the thinning of his mouth, he *had* heard every word.

Mottford Hall Stables
Fifteen minutes later

ARMS FOLDED AND GRATEFUL FOR THE COOL interior of the stables, Theran rested his shoulder against the stall's planked wall. Today promised to be a scorcher, and he looked forward to the boat race. It was always cooler on the water. A swim afterward might be in order, too, though that wasn't on the official list of activities for the house party.

Too bad he hadn't thought to procure a swimming costume for Bernadine. He could've begun her swimming lessons. Unable to prevent the half-smile stretching his mouth, he regarded his entranced daughter.

At first demonstrating typical maternal protective behavior, once the Dalmatian realized there was no threat to her puppies, Preta settled onto her side. Emitting little squeals and whines, the ten pups wriggled and rooted about until they seized a teat, then nursed feverishly.

Little piglets.

Remarkably well behaved, the children sat quietly in a circle, legs crossed, and waited their turn to pet one of the three-week-old puppies. Bernadine's face shone with happiness as she cooed and whispered to the tiny pup. Every now and again, she glanced toward the other puppies, her attention always focusing on the smallest one.

Theran made eye contact with Enos—the head groom—and covertly handed him a yellow ribbon.

"The runt," Theran said.

Enos grunted his understanding.

Theran had already asked his aunt and uncle if Bernadine might have a pup. They readily agreed, as he'd known they would. Two kinder people he'd never known. His mother, Melvelia's sister, had a stubborn streak his aunt lacked.

Aunt Melvelia had procured a length of ribbon from her sewing basket. "Have Enos tie it around the puppy's neck to identify it as Bernadine's," she advised.

Grinning and revealing a missing front tooth, Enos nodded as he tucked the ribbon into his pocket.

"Lucky lassie," he said beneath his breath. "The bairns will be weaned end of September."

Just in time for Bernadine's birthday, October fourth.

Pulling his cap from his head and wiping his forehead with his forearm, the head groom jutted his chin toward the mother. "Preta is young—barely a year old herself—but she's a natural mother. Not all females are, ye ken."

"I'll say not," dared one of the maids, with a saucy smile. "Half don't know what to do with theirs, and the other half cannot be bothered with them."

She wasn't referring to animals. Neither was she wrong.

Miss Mayfield squatted beside a little girl, and a strange look flitted across her features. She shifted her attention to Preta. A stricken—*guilty?*—expression had chased her warm smile away when she'd lifted her head and spied him after Bernadine's enthusiastic declaration.

He'd have to speak with his daughter about Miss Mayfield and explain why the governess couldn't become her mother.

A horse snorted in a stall, and another whuffed a response. Outside, birds chirped and tweeted. In the distance, a man shouted, and a woman laughed. The welcome breeze passing from the open doors on one end of the stables to the other carried the tangy aromas of sweet hay, oats, liniment, and fresh manure.

No more than five or six, a dark-haired waif wrinkled her nose before pinching it with her thumb and forefinger. "*Pee-ew.*"

Snickers broke out as more children did the same.

"Stinky pooh."

"Pee-ew."

"Poopy poop."

"That's enough, children," Miss Mayfield gently admonished. "We do not discuss unpleasant smells."

Bernadine climbed to her feet and made her way to Theran. He lifted her onto his shoulders. She giggled and clutched his head. Chuckling, he guided her little hands to the side of his head and not over his eyes.

"We should return to the house, children. We must prepare to watch the boat races," the other governess, whom Theran did not know, announced.

Now there was proper governess material.

Her thick eyebrows grew together across a large nose, which balanced a pair of thick spectacles. When she smiled—which she did often—her slightly bucked teeth gave her the appearance of a happy rabbit. As broad at the shoulders as she was at the hips, in her burlap-brown gown, she rather resembled a potato. Though no hairs protruded from her chin, a pea-sized mole upon her right cheek did.

All in all, the perfect specimen of a governess.

In every way, the opposite of the green-eyed goddess who'd upended Theran's comfortable existence.

He caught himself.

Goddess?

Now he waxed nonsensical.

He blamed his ridiculous musings on his lack of sleep. Theran had tossed and turned in his overheated room, visions of Miss Mayfield fighting off Lord Ceddes disrupting all attempts to drift into slumber. Not to mention the urge he'd almost indulged to kiss her. His pillow had taken a beating as he'd pounded and thumped the innocent padding in an attempt to get comfortable and to put her from his mind.

It was better when they were at odds, as they had been since that first day.

Now that he'd held her soft, womanly form in his arms, he couldn't forget the feel of her rounded curves. Her clean fragrance with the merest hint of citrus.

Miss Mayfield straightened and handed Enos the pup. "Thank you."

"Yer welcome, lass." He placed the whimpering pup with his anxious mother, who proceeded to lick him thoroughly.

"I have a foal to check on. Excuse me." Lifting a finger to his forehead in a silent salute, Enos departed.

With a practiced eye, Miss Mayfield regarded the boys and girls as they rose and brushed the hay and dust from their clothing. "Our hosts have provided each of you with your very own sailboat for the boat races this morning."

That announcement met with squeals of delight and a few joyous bounces. How sad that soon, these natural and exuberant emotions would likely be quashed by a stodgy tutor, fusty governess, or stern teacher. Or worse yet, a disapproving parent.

Which made finding the right governess for Bernadine so critical. One who wouldn't stifle her *joie de vivre*—joy of life— but assist her in developing her natural abilities and talents.

"Might I have a word with you, Miss Mayfield?" Theran said as he swung Bernadine to the floor.

Her crescent lashes swept to her ivory cheeks for a moment as if she needed to bolster her courage. Theran couldn't fault her for her reluctance to parry with him. He admitted he'd not been at his best with her.

Pinning a professional smile on her lips, she gave a brisk nod. "Of course. Caitya, could you please take Bernadine to the house for me? I'll be but a few minutes."

"I'd be happy to," the Irish maid responded with a broad smile as she held her hand out to Bernadine. "Come, love."

"I don't want to." Thrusting her lower lip out, Bernadine pouted. "I want to stay with you and Miss Mayfield, Papa."

Defiance wasn't typical for his daughter. Theran was a loving father but expected respect and obedience.

"Not now, Bernadine. The boat races commence shortly, and I have something of import to discuss with Miss Mayfield. Go with Caitya." He turned her toward the waiting servant. "I shall see you at the shore in a short while."

"Go along, Bernadine," Miss Mayfield encouraged. "You must pick a color for your sailboat's sail still."

"Yellow," Bernadine said without hesitation as she skipped beside the maid.

Last year, everything had been pink.

That prompted calls from the other children about what color their sails would be.

Miss Mayfield observed the laughing, chatting children and their trio of cheerful chaperones exiting the building before facing Theran.

He was still trying to formulate a tactful way of telling Miss Mayfield to discourage Bernadine's childish fantasy of him marrying her. Today, Miss Mayfield wore a gray gown, which turned her eyes a stormy-sea color.

Did the shade change with what she wore?

She offered a ghost of a smile, an uneasiness lingering in

the depths of her turbulent gaze. "I want to thank you for allowing me to act as Bernadine's governess for the rest of the house party, Mr. Rutland. It was unexpected and very generous of you."

Blast and rot.

Theran cupped his nape and floundered for a way to extricate himself from the awkward predicament his aunt had put him in.

"Ah, I see." Head tilted, Miss Mayfield peered up at him. She curved her plump, plum-tinted lips into a wry arc.

She'd figured it out.

Clever, intelligent girl.

"*You* didn't make the offer. Your aunt did." Her gaze sank to the scuffed wooden floor for a heartbeat then she met his gaze straight on. Only her fingers clenching the folds of her gown betrayed her tension.

"Would you prefer I refuse your aunt's kind offer, Mr. Rutland?"

FOURTEEN

I think it would be a very grand thing indeed if you and your husband were to come for a Christmastide house party. I have invited the Morrisettes and several of our friends from Haven House and Academy for the Enrichment of Young Women. Duties may prevent all of them from attending, but I want them to feel welcome. Several of Ronan's friends will round out the guest list.

Trinity Ablethorne has returned to England. I so look forward to hearing about her grand adventures abroad.

Do say you'll attempt to come.

~Mercy Brockman, in an invitation
to Chasity Terramier

Still Mottford Hall Stables

Well, that would make Theran out to be the biggest bloody

ponce and ogre of all time, wouldn't it? To deny a sacked governess a couple weeks more income?

Bernadine would be crushed as well.

"No." Theran shook his head. "I see no harm in continuing for the present. I don't intend to stay at the house party the entire time in any event." Beyond the barn, a stable hand exercised White Flame. Theran had missed his usual morning ride, and a slight restlessness plagued him as a result. "My brother's wife is expecting their third child soon, and he and my mother would like me there."

"How wonderful." A soft, maternal smile bloomed across Purity's face, once again startling him with her vivacity.

Was it only a day ago that he'd first seen her and thought her unremarkable? Purity Mayfield reminded him of a flower bud, breathtaking in its splendor when fully opened.

And she was meant to be a mother. She wouldn't leave her children for someone else to raise. Wouldn't neglect them for her own self-interests. She'd nurture and love and discipline and praise them.

Imogene had been that kind of mother.

The queerest emotion burbled behind Theran's ribs and rose to the back of his throat. Not regret that Imogen wouldn't be that sort of mother for Bernadine, but at the very real probability that Purity would never bear her own children. Many women in service didn't. Survival in an unforgiving world didn't permit the luxury of motherhood.

How could Theran deny Bernadine a governess who would love her like her own child?

"I am at your disposal for as long as you require," she said demurely.

A stark contrast to the feisty woman who'd given him an earful only a couple of days ago and the woman who'd fought off Lord Ceddes' lecherous attentions last night.

Aunt Melvelia was right.

Hiring Miss Mayfield was the perfect solution.

You've already sent Spottswood a letter asking him to post the position.

Easy enough to write him again and rescind the directive.

This is a mistake.

"You wished to speak to me about something, Mr. Rutland?" Though she refrained from looking to where the children had disappeared, Purity subtly shifted her weight toward the door. He appreciated her impatience to return to her charge. More credit to her for her commitment to her duty.

Athena had frequently neglected her duties.

Ah, yes. Theran needed to write his sister-in-law and ensure that she understood he would take personally any future threats against Purity. And deal with them swiftly and appropriately.

"I did." He cleared his throat. "I have... that is...would you...?"

Bother and blast.

He stumbled over his words like an inexperienced, pimple-faced schoolboy asking the girl he was infatuated with to dance.

"Would I...?"

Guileless and unassuming, Purity's gaze searched his face.

Could she truly be as genuine and unaffected as she appeared?

Don't do it, Theran Marcus Anthony Rutland.

You shall regret it.

Aye, he probably would.

Even as his conscience silently berated him, Theran said, "Would you consider accepting the position as Bernadine's governess?"

"Would I...?"

He'd completely flummoxed Purity.

She gave a slight shake of her dark head. No impetuous curl sprang free today, more was the pity. She had glorious hair. Thick and luxurious like a mink but teeming with curls a man longed to comb his fingers through.

"Forgive me. Are you suggesting a position that lasts beyond the house party?"

He cursed inwardly at the tiny spark of hope in her gorgeous eyes and the inflection in her voice she couldn't disguise.

"I am."

Though the devil on his shoulder screamed he'd come to regret it. "At twice the wages you received from the Ceddes. These next weeks can act as a probationary period. If things go well, then we can discuss a lengthy contract."

It was done, then.

Theran had become a full-blown, besotted imbecile.

No, not besotted. Merely willing to do whatever was necessary to give his daughter the best upbringing he could provide, and Purity Mayfield was clearly critical to that endeavor.

At least for now.

Then why did he have the overwhelming yearning to take her into his arms and kiss her until they were both breathless? To nuzzle the silken column of her throat and run his tongue over the shell of her ear?

"Even knowing I am a person of faith?" Purity ventured with an air of confidence.

That cooled his arduous musings.

"I don't perceive your beliefs as an impediment." She wouldn't throw herself at him and beg him to take her as

Athena had. A virtuous woman helping raise his daughter might be a boon.

Theran shrugged then picked off a bit of hay Bernadine must've left on his sleeve when he'd picked her up. "I do ask that you restrain from unduly influencing Bernadine. When she reaches an age of understanding and maturity, she can make those choices for herself."

Purity remained silent for several seconds. So long, in truth, he believed she'd decline the offer. She suddenly graced him with one of her blinding smiles. Not the practiced, professional upward tilt of her mouth, but the unrestrained expression of happiness.

"I accept."

"Excellent." Theran couldn't decide if the knot in his belly was relief that he'd found a suitable governess or anxiety that he'd made a monumental mistake. "I shall have my man of affairs draft a contract."

"As you wish, though I am content to wait until the probationary period is over."

Aunt Melvelia would be beside herself with excitement.

Hiring an attractive governess—one whom Theran had already admitted, if only to himself, that he desired—was not prudent.

Bollocks.

He was more than capable of controlling his baser urges. Besides, midnight swims in freezing ponds awaited if his body refused to adhere to the directives of his mind.

"I'll see you at the boat races and picnic, I presume," Purity asked as she turned toward the exit.

"Yes. I'm racing with two chums."

What time was it anyway?

After he'd stood them up for cricket, Everingham and Hemsworth would be vexed if he was late.

"I shall see you then, Mr. Rutland." She paused, the bright light from the open door illuminating her silhouette with an ethereal glow. She looked angelic. "Thank you."

Her gratitude eviscerated him, cleaved his hardened heart in two.

What must it be like to be dependent upon the good graces of others? To monitor every word and censure every action to ensure continued favor and employment? He'd never known poverty or want. As the privileged third son of a lord, his path had been paved with comfort and wealth.

Theran merely made a noise in his throat, his attention on the innocent, alluring sway of her hips as Purity departed.

"God above, what have I done?" he mumbled to himself.

A horse in a nearby stall whinnied...a distinctly mocking horsey laugh.

Only after Purity had disappeared from sight did Theran remember he'd never asked her to correct Bernadine about the impossibility of her becoming his wife.

FIFTEEN

I regret the nature of our parting, Miss Mayfield. My children are quite devastated. Despite what you may think, I love them, and their grief pains me.

Toward that end, I intend to forward their addresses to you once they are settled in school. I would count it a personal favor if you corresponded with them. They adore you, and I believe you also hold them in great affection.

After a tour of the continent with my sister, I intend to make Petherwick Court my permanent residence. I shall ensure your belongings and wages owed, in addition to a well-deserved bonus, are forwarded to your new lodgings. I have also provided you with a letter of reference.

Please respond with your address at your earliest convenience.

~Odelia Bardslay, Viscountess Ceddes,
to Miss Purity Mayfield in a hastily
scribbled note while waiting for the
coach to carry her family
from Mottford Hall

. . .

Path from the stables to the Mottford Hall terrace
Five minutes later

Purity couldn't keep the bounce from her step as she hurried back to the house. She had no idea what had changed Mr. Rutland's mind about hiring her as Bernadine's governess, but it was an answer to prayer, to be sure.

True, Purity knew little about Theran Rutland: he loved his daughter; he was intimidating when angry; his name had set Viscount Ceddes to quaking.

And he has strapping legs, arms like iron, devilish blue eyes, and he smells heavenly.

The unsolicited thought slashed into her musings as she marched along, stirring undecipherable yearning. Mayhap she understood Athena Sommerville's infatuation the merest bit.

Not that Purity was enamored. She was not.

Only a nitwit permitted her feelings to become engaged in a futile, fruitless unrequited fascination. Merely days ago, Mr. Rutland had accused her of being a gossip and a liar.

Regardless, his aunt held him in the highest regard, and the countess was the epitome of kindness and decency. If the position turned out to be an impossible fit, if Purity and Mr. Rutland didn't suit, she still had Chasity's invitation to fall back on as well as applying for a position at Balderbrook's Institution for Genteel Ladies.

A tiny jolt of sadness impinged upon her happiness as she strode the path.

She had wanted to attend Chasity's wedding to Aston Terramier and Mercy's to Ronan Brockman. But it had been infeasible. Not only had the Ceddes never given her more than half a day off at any given time, but this house party was also the last time she'd see the children she'd cared for these past eight years.

She'd miss the Bardslay children, but she had a new charge now. An energetic, intelligent, strong-minded, but sweet-natured little girl. With an impossibly handsome, enigmatic widower for a father.

A smile teasing her lips, Purity slipped into the house. In short order, she entered her bedchamber, removed her bonnet, and hung it up on a hook. A closed valise sat upon one of the other beds.

A roommate had arrived while she'd been in the stables.

Standing before the small cheval mirror, she pinned a few unruly curls back into her knot as she stared at her countenance. She'd never given much consideration to her parentage or her appearance.

Hands on her hips, she took an impartial assessment. Her mouth was a bit too small, and her nose a trifle too long. A nice slope to her cheekbones, but her chin was a smidgeon too bold. All in all, her eyes were her best features. Still, in comparison to Athena Sommerville and the other beauties she'd seen at the house party, Purity was only passably pretty.

Had she inherited her green eyes from her mother or father?

Her height?

Her temperament?

All Mrs. Shepherd could tell her was that she'd come to the foundling home as a toddler. Unlike many of her friends who'd arrived as infants, Purity had spent time with her parents—or someone—before being cast off. Sadly, she hadn't a single memory of them.

A wisp of white on the night table beside her bed, reflected in the looking glass, caught her eye.

What was that?

She slipped a fingernail beneath the wax seal and hitched her breath when a second sheet of foolscap slipped free. Purity caught the neatly folded rectangle in her other hand, then skimmed the missive.

Wonder of wonders.

She almost laughed out loud in relief.

Lady Ceddes had taken the time to pen her a note before she departed. Her ladyship wanted Purity to write the children. She'd also provided the coveted letter of reference.

Purity carefully unfolded the letter, and tears blurred her eyes.

The viscountess had written a flattering recommendation.

Just that morning, Purity had fretted what she was going to do, and now she not only had a letter of reference, she'd found a position.

Well, it had found her thanks to Lady Mumford.

The door swung open, and Purity turned.

"Trinity?"

"Purity?"

Laying the letters aside, Purity rushed to her girlhood friend, and they embraced.

"I didn't know you would be here," she said. "And we are to room together. How marvelous."

Trinity laughed, her pale blue eyes shining with excitement and joy. "My tenure with Mrs. Westcott ended a few weeks ago. I am now companion to Mrs. Parmelia Templemore."

Purity held her friend's hands. "This is just too splendid. I wish I could stay and chat, but my new ward awaits me. We're off to watch the boat races. Her papa is competing."

Trinity bussed Purity's cheek. "We'll have weeks to catch up in the evenings. Mrs. Templemore retires early, as I imagine your charge does."

"Indeed." Purity gave a little wave as she left the bedchamber.

What a marvelous day this was turning out to be.

The lake's shore
Eleven of the clock

"LOOK, BERNADINE. THERE'S YOUR PAPA."

Holding a parasol borrowed from the countess, Purity pointed to a skiff in the middle of the lake. Her hostess had anticipated the weather and had provided parasols for anyone who required one.

As Purity didn't own a parasol and Bernadine had the fair skin redheads often did, she'd opted to take advantage of Lady Mumford's generosity.

Disgruntled quacking and honking filled the air as displaced waterfowl either waddled onto the shore or retreated to the lake's farthest shore. None were so discontent as to fly away, however. They knew a good thing when it came their way, as did the daily treat of dried bread crumbs.

The gentlemen had removed their coats; a few, including Mr. Rutland, their waistcoats and cravats as well. Each of the six boats held three competitors. With their sleeves rolled to their elbows, they laughed and jested as the chattering guests made themselves comfortable on the shore in preparation for the race.

Bernadine held the string connected to her sailboat— complete with its sunny, yellow sail—floating at the lake's edge. Standing on her tiptoes, she waved to her father. The welcome breeze ruffled her pink gown and her matching bonnet's ribbon.

Somehow in the crowd teeming along the shore, he saw her and waved back.

Someone sounded a horn, and the boaters took their seats. Two men would row, and the third sat in the stern, calling directions. Mr. Rutland was rowing. No great surprise there, as Purity had already determined from his muscular build that the man was a bit of a Corinthian.

A second horn echoed, and the crowd settled into a hush of anticipation. Even Purity found her pulse beating faster than usual, her gaze fixed on Mr. Rutland's vessel.

"Purty, I cannot see Papa anymore."

A few of the older children had crowded the shore to float their boats as well.

"I'll lift you up." Somehow, Purity managed to lift Bernadine, clutching her dripping sailboat, and still balance the parasol over their heads. "You must remember to address me as Miss Mayfield, dearest."

"Even when you're my mama?" Her green eyes sparkled with hope.

Purity must put an end to this misunderstanding at once. With a hasty glance around, she put her mouth near Bernadine's ear.

"Bernadine, you mustn't say that. I cannot be your mother. Only your governess."

"Why?"

A third, longer horn saved Purity from answering.

Amid raucous cheers from the onlookers, the boats slid forward in the water. Straightaway, two of the craft crashed into one another, sending three gentlemen into the water.

The crowd laughed, jeered, and hooted.

"Go, Papa. Go," Bernadine cheered, waving her toy boat in the air.

In third place, Theran's craft surged forward. Purity tried not to notice the way his muscles bunched and flexed beneath his dampened shirt each time he pulled upon the oars. His hair had fallen forward onto his forehead, giving him a roguish, boyish look.

"I do believe they might win this year," the Countess of Mumford said near Purity's elbow.

Purity started, her heart vaulting to her throat. Had her ladyship heard Bernadine's innocent question?

Lord, Purity hoped not.

"Theran hasn't participated since..." Lady Mumford's kindly gaze shifted to Bernadine, and her ladyship arched a telling eyebrow.

Since his wife had died.

Theran must've loved her deeply. Which explained why he was so very angry with God.

"I want down now, please." Bernadine wiggled and kicked her heels.

Purity lowered the child, and she ran to greet three other little girls nearby.

"How long ago?" Purity wanted to know because it might help her as governess to Bernadine.

"Three years," Lady Mumford answered without hesitation. "Imogene was kind-hearted and sweet-tempered, though she was capable of a tongue lashing if incensed. It devastated Theran when she died shortly after returning from a visit to her father's."

"How awful."

"I shan't pretend it wasn't, but life goes on despite what we endure. Our faith keeps us strong." Her ladyship grew contemplative as she regarded the boats zipping across the lake. "Theran's on the mend now, and it is delightful to see him laughing and enjoying himself once more."

The race had come down to two boats now; the one with Mr. Rutland and another about six feet ahead. The crowd shouted encouragement to their favorites while the rowers strained to pull their craft ahead.

Keeping one eye on Bernadine, Purity shifted the parasol and smiled down at the Countess of Mumford. "Thank you, my lady, for your confidence in me. I hope I shan't disappoint."

"Tish tosh." Her ladyship waved her red lace fan. "I know a gem when I see one, and you, Miss Mayfield, are a gem." She squinted slightly as another boat capsized in the middle of the lake, and after a bit of splashing, three heads bobbed to the surface.

"Mr. Rutland has extended an offer of employment beyond the house party," Purity offered.

Her ladyship gave Purity a side-eyed glance, the merest hint of amusement in her twinkling eyes. "Has he indeed?"

"After a probationary period, that is. To see if we will suit." No, that was not what she meant. "Not Mr. Rutland and me. Bernadine and me."

Stop blathering. You'll only make her suspicious.

"Miss Mayfield, I am hesitant to mention this as I abhor gossip in any form. However, I believe you should be informed."

Purity turned her attention to Lady Mumford.

The countess wore a bemused expression.

"At some point or other, you may hear unsavory rumors about Theran's days as a pugilist," Lady Mumford said. "He was skilled and rather ruthless at the craft and amassed a small fortune from wagers on his matches."

Well, that explained Lord Ceddes's fear when he learned Theran's name.

Waving her fan vigorously to produce a small draft, her ladyship went on, "Theran put that all behind when he and Imogene became betrothed, but unfortunately, the reputation he earned still occasionally casts a black shadow over him."

"Thank you for telling me. His exceptional skills proved quite useful in dispatching Lord Ceddes," Purity quipped with a wry smile. She had no doubt Lady Mumford knew what happened with his lordship.

"Oh, look!" Lady Mumford cried as the spectators exploded into claps and cheers. "Hurrah! I say, he's done it!"

Purity inspected the far shore.

Sure enough, Mr. Rutland's boat had reached the other side first. Frightened waterfowl squawked their objections as they waddled up the embankment or flew across the lake's shimmering surface.

He and the other men in his boat laughed and clapped each other on the back. In their exuberance, they failed to stay in the center of the skiff, and they toppled sideways into the lake.

The onlookers roared with laughter, and even Purity giggled.

As Mr. Rutland came to the surface, he raised a victorious fist in the air.

The crowd thundered all the louder.

"Come, sit with me, Miss Mayfield."

It wasn't as much a suggestion as a command.

Nonetheless, Purity hesitated. "But, Bernadine...?"

"Delphine? Forsythia?" With a wave of her gloved hand, the countess caught the attention of her two youngest daughters standing a few feet away. Each wore gowns that appeared more like a chef's elaborate confection than a seamstress's creation.

"Be dears, and mind Bernadine for a spell, will you?" the countess asked. "Perhaps a game of Simon Says to entertain the children?"

"Of course, Mama," Delphine agreed with a ready smile. "Bernadine, let's play Simon Says, shall we? You may bring your boat if you wish. I'm sure a few of the other children will want to play too."

The girls gathered several other children and led them to an uncluttered lawn area.

"You needn't fret, Miss Mayfield," Lady Mumford assured her. "My daughters will keep an eye on Bernadine. They are very responsible."

"I've no doubt they are." Purity bent her mouth upward even as she unintentionally searched the far shore for a certain raven head. "I feel derelict in my duties, nonetheless."

"He'll have to bathe and change before he rejoins us for the picnic," the Countess of Mumford said, distinct jollity coloring her voice.

Purity wrinkled her forehead. "Who will?"

"La, child. I have eyes in my head." Her ladyship chuckled, sending the bevy of cerulean-blue, gold, and Pompeian-red feathers in her coiffeur trembling. "You cannot take yours off him, and he, alas, is no better than you."

Heat prickled Purity's cheeks.

She refused to ask which *him* the countess referred to.

She hadn't been staring at Theran.

Had she?

"I'm sure you are mistaken, my lady."

Why, Purity managed to sound quite normal. In no way did she give away the bevy of butterflies that had taken to flight in her stomach.

The very idea. It was preposterous. Ludicrous. Nonsensical twaddle.

Theran staring at her, indeed.

Only, Lady Mumford wasn't the flibbertigibbet, whimsical sort.

An amused smile bending her mouth and an arch eyebrow raised high on her forehead, her ladyship looped her hand through Purity's bent elbow and guided her toward a tent erected over several chairs and tables.

"We have at least thirty minutes for you to convince me of that, my dear."

SIXTEEN

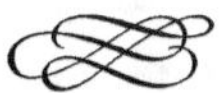

I'm sure you understand the delicacy of the situation, as do I. I have no wish to impose further distress upon you. I believe it would be convenient for everyone if you simply forwarded Miss Mayfield's correspondence and possessions to Mottford Hall until such time as she has a permanent address.

Might I also suggest you inform your staff of the need for circumspection to ensure the delivery of Miss Mayfield's posts?

~Melvelia Hawtrey, Countess of Mumford,
in a discreet note to Odelia Bardslay,
Viscountess Ceddes, before she
departed from Mottford Hall

Mottsford Hall Greens
Twenty minutes later

Having bathed and donned dry clothing with alacrity he didn't want to examine, Theran trotted down the terrace steps. It had been a long while since anticipation had thrummed through his veins. It had nothing to do with Bernadine's new governess, he sternly told himself.

Winning the boat race contributed to his enthusiasm, as well as an eagerness to sample the scrumptious food spread upon half a dozen tables. Nothing like a bit of physical exertion to whet one's appetite.

Plus, an excursion was planned to the ancient abbey on the estate's far side, past the woods this afternoon. The crumbling twelfth-century ruins, still majestic centuries later, never ceased to intrigue. Theran's fascination with historical architecture came only second to his interest in agriculture. As a younger son, he'd been permitted the freedom to pursue his interests. Many—*most*—people were not so fortunate.

Coattails flapping, Theran strode across the lawn. He took in the guests playing shuttlecock or pall mall, strolling the rolling lawns, or enjoying the feast under one of several tents. A few had taken advantage of the boats, and gentlemen languidly rowed across the lake, a lady with her parasol in the bow.

Aunt Melvelia was famous far and wide for her picnics. Even neighbors who weren't staying at the house had accepted the invitation.

No sign of Everingham or Hemsworth yet. Those rogues were probably sipping brandy while lolling in a warm bath with suds to their chins.

He spotted Bernadine on a blanket with Forsythia and Delphine, along with three other teenage girls. They chatted gaily as they ate, frequently giggling at some witticism or other. Amaryllis and her friends sat in chairs a few feet away, evidently too grown-up for sitting on a blanket anymore.

Where was Purity?

Since when had Theran begun thinking of her by her given name?

He must keep their arrangement strictly business. To do otherwise could lend itself to a myriad of complications.

As he maneuvered through guests, he returned nods of greeting and acknowledged congratulations. For the first time in a long while, he became aware of the subtle, coy invitations sent in his direction by ladies interested in a romantic interlude: A tongue trailed across a lower lip. A hand casually brushed over a full bosom. A sultry-eyed wink. A brazen stare at his nether regions followed by a vixen's smile.

God save him from wanton women.

Grief had kept him from attending social affairs for three years, and before that, he'd only had eyes for his wife.

Theran turned his mouth downward in distaste.

Even before he'd married, trysts with married women had never appealed. They did even less now that he'd experienced the joys of matrimony. Marriage vows were sacred and not to be disregarded at the slightest whim or wave of lust.

Ah, there was Purity with her back to him, sitting with his aunt and uncle not far from where Bernadine enjoyed her luncheon. She'd angled herself to observe Bernadine but still permit his daughter a degree of independence.

He permitted himself a moment's lazy contemplation as he closed the distance.

What was it about this woman that beckoned him?

Purity looked nothing like Imogene except her green eyes, and even those weren't the same shade of green. Imogene had been just over five feet tall. Purity was several inches taller. Where Imogene's figure had been voluptuous and generous, Purity's womanly curves were lithe and willowy.

Purity worked for a living while Imogene had never toiled

a day in her life except for activities she enjoyed. Naturally, Purity must be well-educated and likely well-read. Imogene had attended finishing school, but no one would ever have called her a bluestocking.

So what was this potent allure to the governess Theran had met a few days ago?

This appeal that stirred or perhaps awakened a dormant part of his soul?

Something undecipherable, undefinable, about Purity Mayfield whispered to his own wounded spirit.

And he'd stupidly hired her as his daughter's governess.

Talk about a fox in the chicken coop, but *he* was the fox.

His aunt spotted Theran first and waved an exuberant invitation. "Theran. Do join us."

At his aunt's call, Purity glanced over her shoulder.

Their eyes met, and her lips swept upward before she averted her gaze in characteristic subservience.

His heart kicked into a new rhythm—perplexing and provocative.

"Well done, Theran." Uncle Herbert offered a hearty handshake. "I thought Bardstone and his crew had you. Indeed, I did. But that surge at the end propelled you ahead to a brilliant finish. Too bad about that topple into the lake afterward."

Everyone chuckled.

Bernadine gave him a merry wave but seemed disinclined to leave the older girls. Probably because they were spoiling her with attention.

He waved back.

His aunt's merry gaze fairly sparkled. "I specifically asked Cook to prepare Scotch eggs and smoked salmon. I know they are favorites of yours."

"Have I told you lately that you're my favorite aunt?" Kissing the back of her hand, Theran winked.

"Pshaw." Aunt Melvelia slapped his forearm with her fan. "Pretty words to be sure, but as I'm your only aunt, you'll have to do better than that."

"She has you there, my boy," Uncle Herbert said, casting his wife an affectionate glance.

"Miss Mayfield, why don't you go along with Theran and fill a plate yourself?" his aunt suggested with the subtlety of a drunken kangaroo in a tiara hopping about a parlor. "You've not eaten yet, so diligently have you monitored Bernadine."

"Oh, I couldn't." Purity shook her head and met his gaze for a second before dutifully returning her regard to Bernadine. "I'll eat later. I'm accustomed to doing so."

Athena had never denied herself a meal—or anything for that matter—in favor of her responsibilities to Bernadine.

"Bernadine is quite safe at the moment, Miss Mayfield. I don't think there is any harm in you enjoying the delicious food while it is fresh." Theran extended his hand.

She stared at it for a long second, indecision warring in her gaze.

He bent over and whispered, "I won't bite, I promise."

That propelled her to her feet with a distinct pinkish tint to her cheeks.

"I shan't be more than five minutes," she said to no one in particular.

As they wended their way to the groaning tables, Theran asked, "Have you attended many house parties?"

"Lord, no." Purity laughed and sobered almost as quickly with a swift, self-conscious glance around.

She disguised it well, but she fretted about what others thought. Even the hint of impropriety could be grounds for dismissal.

"This is my first. The Ceddes seldom visited their children, and during my eight years with them, this was the first time they'd attended any function as a family."

Eight years.

That would make Purity…What? In her late twenties?

They reached the tables, and a footman handed them each a plate.

"How can I possibly decide?" Purity took in the enormous selection of food.

For a moment, Theran was ashamed of the opulence he took for granted.

"You must try the Scotch eggs." He placed one on her plate. "Have you ever had them before?"

Purity shook her head.

"They're boiled eggs, wrapped in sausage, then rolled in breadcrumbs and fried. They've been a favorite of mine since childhood."

"Do you have Scots in your ancestry?" she asked, placing a fat strawberry followed by a hot cross bun on her plate.

"Aye, though it's three generations back," he said with a mock brogue.

A slightly faraway look entered her eyes. "I know nothing about my family."

Theran nodded at the footman offering a piece of sliced beef.

"I'm sorry, Purity."

She glanced up at him and raised a delicate shoulder. "You needn't be. I was raised by a loving, caring woman, surrounded by girls I consider more sisters than friends. I was blessed with a benefactor who cared enough to place me in a home. Many are not so fortunate as I."

Theran's esteem for Purity elevated even further. Rather

than feeling sorry for herself, she accepted her fate and even considered herself blessed.

Blessed.

When was the last time Theran counted his blessings rather than his losses or disappointments?

Soon, their plates overflowing with succulent foods, they carefully picked their way between picnickers back to his aunt and uncle.

"There's an excursion to an abbey's ruins later this afternoon." Theran gave Purity a sideways glance. "Would you like to go along?"

"I...what time?" She puzzled her brow beneath her bonnet. "Bernadine naps in the afternoon, though I suppose she might miss one day with your permission."

"I meant without her." Theran had lost his bloody mind, and yet his mouth kept rattling on. Like a runaway carriage plummeting downhill. "The ruins are no place for a curious child."

"Oh. Then, I don't think so, Mr. Rutland, though I thank you for the invitation." Her smile contained a rueful tilt. "That would undoubtedly cause whispers. I'm already the object of speculation."

Well, at least one of them had a degree of common sense left. Theran's seemed to have departed with the sunrise. He suspected it might not return anytime soon.

They'd reached his aunt and uncle.

"Theran, a letter arrived by messenger for you from Trenthurst House." Aunt Melvelia indicated the rectangle lying upon the white tablecloth. "Kebble said it was urgent."

Worry lines etched her forehead.

After setting his plate down, Theran broke the seal and swiftly perused the contents.

"Forgive me, but I must leave at once. Violetta delivered the babe prematurely." Pain scissored his stomach as he put a hand to his forehead. "They aren't certain either will live."

SEVENTEEN

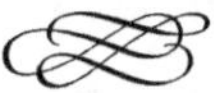

You must come at once.

Violetta delivered a daughter early this morning, over a month early. The physician fears for her life and the infant's. Jordan is beside himself, and Raymond is still at sea as far as we know. Your brother needs you.

~Celena Rutland, in a frantic note
to her youngest son, Theran Rutland

Dartford, England
A bumpy stretch of road four miles from Trenthurst
Hose
Five Hours Later

Purity rested her head against the coach's sky-blue squabs in a futile attempt to sleep. Bernadine lay on the opposite seat, knees tucked to her chest, slumbering soundly. Children always managed to sleep during difficult times. Adults,

145

however, had minds that refused to turn off troublesome monologues.

For instance, why had Theran invited her to tour the abbey's ruins?

Why had Purity's body gone hot, then cold, then hot again when she'd spied him crossing the greens in long, sleek strides?

Had it really only been three days since she'd met Theran Rutland?

He had her at sixes and sevens.

One moment he was kind and patient and the next disdainful and inflexible.

Purity's bonnet, gloves, and spencer lay on the seat beside her. The heat inside the coach's interior didn't lend itself to extra garments. Even now, moisture dampened her temples and underarms. She dabbed her face with a handkerchief, vacillating between wishing they'd reach their destination and dreading doing so.

Rather than travel inside the coach, Theran rode White Flame. Probably as much to transport the horse to Trenthurst House as to burn off his agitation. Sitting in a carriage for several hours didn't lend itself to lessening tension, as she could well attest to.

Another possibility existed for why he'd ridden instead of joining his daughter and her new governess within the coach: to give the appearance of respectability.

Likely, it was a combination of all three reasons. Purity appreciated the gesture, even if it wasn't required. He hadn't thought it necessary to protect her reputation that day in his aunt's salon, so what had changed?

Sighing, she shifted positions and gave up on sleeping.

What she wouldn't give for a hand fan, but governesses had little use for such an accessory. Instead, she ineffectually waved her handkerchief before her face. She'd lowered the windows some time ago but kept the shades partially closed to prevent road dust from caking everything inside the conveyance.

The well-sprung coach lumbered along, squeaking and groaning when it dipped into a hole. The wheels ground away in a soothing rhythm as they rolled across the rutted road. This conveyance was loftier than the coach she and the Bardslay children had at their disposal but not luxurious as the Ceddes' viscountcy coach.

With a start, Purity realized this was the farthest she'd ever traveled.

My, how her life had changed in a few short days.

She hadn't hesitated when Theran had asked if she could be ready to depart within the hour.

What else could she have done?

The question of whether she'd remain Bernadine's governess after the house party was moot. She'd just have to prove herself and convince Theran that not only was she qualified, but she was also a good fit for Bernadine.

Purity studied the slumbering child. Cheeks flushed and mouth parted, Bernadine dreamed on.

Somehow, she needed to persuade the imp that she couldn't be her mother. However, that might be easier said than done. Once a notion took root in a child's head, particularly a bright, strong-willed child, extricating that idea might take a while.

While the conveyance trundled along, Purity poured herself a half glass of lukewarm water. Regardless, it quenched her thirst and refreshed her a jot as well. Lady Mumford had sent along a basket with enough food and beverages to feed them for a week. She'd also confided that she'd asked Lady Ceddes to send Purity's possessions to Mottford Hall. When they arrived, the Countess of Mumford promised to have them delivered to Trenthurst House.

A wry smile tipped up the edges of Purity's mouth.

If she were still there.

Her belongings might well follow her from house to house to house. It was a good thing she'd packed for a month-long house party.

The coach slowed to a jerky stop, and she leaned forward to see out the window.

A lush green field dotted with black-faced sheared sheep greeted her on the right. Lining the road to the left stood a towering grove of gnarled oaks, behind which marched a dry-stone fence. The most curious-looking cattle—black except for a white band around their middles—milled about a stream burbling through the partially shaded meadow.

Why had the coach halted?

They'd changed the team of horses an hour before, and both she and Bernadine, after sampling the delicious foods in the basket, had frequented the necessary behind the rustic inn. That part of traveling Purity could well do without.

The coach door swung open, and a blast of welcome fresh air billowed inside.

Bliss.

Theran poked his head through the opening and slanted his mouth into a disarming smile. With a fond glance at his slumbering daughter, he removed his jacket.

"I'll sit beside you. I don't wish to waken Bernadine just yet."

Purity dutifully gathered her belongings and placed them on her lap with her reticule.

"We'll be at Trenthurst House within the quarter-hour," he said, folding onto the bench beside Purity. At once, the warmth of his body radiated to her.

He smelled of horse, sunlight, and slightly of sweat. After laying his jacket and hat near Bernadine's feet, he said, "I thought it prudent to tell you a little about my family before we arrive."

"That's considerate of you." Purity was curious about what to expect. Surely they'd be surprised Miss Sommerville wasn't the governess any longer.

Purity had gone off pell-mell with a man she'd only met a few days before, and their initial meeting had not been cordial. Well, that wasn't precisely true. Sparks hadn't flown until the tense discussion in his aunt's salon.

With a knuckle to the roof to notify the drivers to resume the journey, Theran stretched his long legs out until his dusty Hessians touched the other side.

Purity tried not to notice their sinuous, muscular length covered in fawn pantaloons. She wasn't in the habit of noticing men's physiques, yet from the moment she'd first laid eyes upon Theran approaching on the Mumfords' lawns, she'd noted every detail of his form.

The coach lurched into motion once more, and she fixed her attention on her lap.

Without asking permission, Theran untied his cravat, leaving it hanging from his neck, and unbuttoned his claret and gold waistcoat.

Not a man to stand on formalities, was he?

She couldn't blame him. Inside the coach was sweltering.

In truth, Purity liked that he was comfortable enough to relax around her.

"I'm the youngest of three, all boys. Jordan is the eldest and heir to the Trentchard Viscountcy when our grandfather passes, as Father died eight years ago. Jordan and his wife, Violetta, have two boys: Jeffrey, six; and Landon, four. And now, of course, the new babe."

He frowned then raked his fingers through his damp hair, leaving it slightly tousled. "Mother didn't mention her name."

"Many babes come into the world early and go on to thrive." Purity hoped to encourage him that all was not lost.

In truth, many so-called *early* births resulted from relationships before marriage. Mrs. Shepherd had never shielded her students from the sordid facts of life.

"The more you know about such matters, the better prepared you'll be to face life's challenges," she said. "You do not want your daughters ending up in the same situations you find yourselves."

Castoffs left to be raised in a foundling home and school.

"Your other brother?" Purity prompted when Theran fell into contemplative silence, studying the passing landscape.

"Raymond." He cast her a boyish grin. "He's the proverbial prodigal son. Joined the navy rather than attend university. Rose up in the ranks on his own merit. A rapscallion if there ever was one." He quirked a raven eyebrow. "And a terrible flirt. Best watch yourself around him. He could talk the curl right out of a pig's tail with his glib tongue."

"Did you just compare me to a pig's tail?" Purity hid a smile behind mock offense.

"No...I..."

Theran appeared thoroughly nonplussed for several turns of the coach wheels. A slow grin lit his face, reaching his eyes and creasing them at the corners as if he'd once laughed often. The silver flecks in his indigo-blue irises glinted with amusement.

"Why, Miss Purity Mayfield. Are you jesting with me?"

Her name on his lips, spoken in that smooth baritone, caused her to curl her toes into the soles of her half boots. No man's voice should have that powerful effect on a female.

"I couldn't let the opportunity pass," she said, much more breathless than she'd like to have done.

"Hmm," was all he said, but his enigmatic gaze, lingering a moment too long on her lips, held an unspoken promise of retribution.

Her heart shouldn't flutter in anticipation, but the disloyal thing did just that.

"You'll find my mother a force to reckon with. Aunt Melvelia often refers to her sister as a dervish." Pulling his ear lobe, he grinned, flashing white teeth in a sun-bronzed face. "The term is not without merit. Some might call Mother eccentric. She'll ask you all sorts of meddling questions and try to bully you into answering. I suggest you simply direct her to me."

"I'm not the least intimidated now," Purity murmured, feeling quite the opposite.

"She means no harm." He skewed his mouth into a lopsided smile. "She loves too much, I think, and is fiercely protective of her family."

How could one love too much?

Theran took Purity's hand in his and gave it a little, encouraging squeeze before releasing it. A jolt zipped up her arm and a shiver down her spine at the contact, and the oddest sense of bereftness washed over her at the loss of his touch.

It was the heat.

That was all.

The excitement of a new position and the strain of the rushed journey. Not to mention the sorrowful reasons for the trip. Purity's reaction assuredly wasn't because of a blooming attraction to her new employer.

Theran brushed a speck of dust from his pantaloons, his granite-hard thigh just inches from Purity's own.

Oh, Lord. Purity was in trouble.

No. No, she most emphatically was not.

She had been trained from girlhood on decorum and etiquette. On what was expected from an employee. How to graciously and professionally handle the most challenging of situations. It was simply a matter of setting her mind to the task.

If only her mind wouldn't keep wandering down forbidden paths.

"Just keep that in mind, Purity, when Mother becomes overbearing." He chuckled, the sound echoing in his chest. "I promise, she shall."

His amusement was contagious, and she couldn't prevent her answering grin. "I shall attempt to."

This air of familiarity between them would not do. It was too disconcerting. Too bewildering.

Should Purity ask Theran to stop addressing her by her given name, or was she overreacting? Perhaps because they were alone, he felt comfortable enough to stretch the bounds. He'd never done so in public.

Yes, but look at his garments—how he'd untied his neckcloth without so much as a by your leave.

Her focus caught on the few intriguing midnight hairs peeking from the top of his shirt. Swallowing, she dropped her gaze to her hands clenching her spencer.

Yes, she should say something.

Put things to right and establish an appropriate foundation from the onset. However, before Purity could open her mouth to suggest their interactions remain formal and professional at all times, the carriage swayed to a halt once more.

"We are here," Theran said. His countenance became serious. "Whatever you do, don't mention what happened with Athena. She is a neighbor, and a feud between families never bodes well. Particularly as her stepfather was my father-in-law."

Purity's jaw went slack.

The irrational, raving woman who'd vowed revenge on her lived nearby?

"Miss Sommerville is your brother's neighbor?" she asked, feeling slightly wobbly in her tummy.

Well, that made sense. Miss Sommerville had said she'd known Theran for years.

"Yes. She, her mother, and stepfather—my wife's father owns the property to the west of Trenthurt House. The Marquess of Ballister has an estate to the east. He's a good friend of my brother Jordan."

Theran touched her hand, and that same jolt of awareness sizzled up the length of her arm.

"My aunt told me Athena threatened you." His troubled gaze searched hers. "I won't let anything happen to you, Purity."

He had happened to her, and it was too late to pretend this man hadn't changed the course of her life. Or that he didn't stir feelings in her she ought not to have.

The question was, was it for better or worse?

EIGHTEEN

Trinity, I am so sorry we shan't have our visit, after all. Mr. Rutland has a family emergency, and we left for Dartford, post-haste. Please send your address to Trenthurst House or Atherley Hall so that we might correspond. Lady Mumford has the direction for both.

I have hopes we shall have the opportunity to visit soon. It has been far too long.

~Purity Mayfield, in a note left
on Trinity Ablethorne's bed

Trenthurst House Drawing Room
7 September 1818 –Afternoon

Trenthurst House could literally be crumbling down around them, and Mother would still insist on serving tea at precisely four o'clock. Unpunctuality was considered blasphemous, and due to White Flame throwing a shoe while Theran was riding, he was late. Which meant an imperious brow raised in disfavor.

Still, he couldn't very well arrive smelling of horse and sweat, with filth on his boots. That would get him soundly scolded.

Trenthurst House held so many memories. It was where he'd grown up, where he'd met Imogene, where he'd come when she'd died. Its familiarity was comforting, and Mother doted on Bernadine. In truth, Mother adored all of her grandchildren.

Purity Mayfield had been a godsend. Not only was she patient and organized with respect to Bernadine, but she'd also, without being asked, taken Jeffery and Landon under her wing as well. The children's days were full of outdoor excursions, lessons, playtime, and bedtime stories. Even a baking lesson and training on how to groom a horse.

Purity Mayfield believed in holistic education.

Theran strongly suspected there were bedtime prayers as well, but his antagonism about faith mere weeks ago had lessened. More due, he'd concluded, to his heart and soul finally healing, and *that* was due to a certain green-eyed minx with a winsome smile and witty disposition.

A smile teased the corners of Theran's mouth. He enjoyed time spent with Purity and, more often than not, joined her and the children on their outings. She was as intelligent as he'd suspected but also possessed a delightful sense of humor.

Not adhering to *haut ton* dictates, Mother insisted the children and their governess eat meals with the family. That suited Theran fine as he did the same at Atherley Hall. He found that the more time he spent with Purity, the more time he wanted to spend with her.

And by thunder, his interest was not purely professional.

No, in point of fact, he was falling in love with Purity. He kept the secret close to his chest, savoring the novelty, the newness, and the incredulity that she'd captured his heart.

More than once, Jordan and Mother had asked him where he'd found such a treasure.

Thus far, because of the chaos in the household, Theran had avoided a straight answer. Perhaps if he were fortunate, he'd never have to explain. The truth made both of them seem impetuous and imprudent. Perhaps there was nothing wrong with that.

Raymond hadn't yet arrived, and Theran speculated his brother mightn't at all, despite his letter of a few weeks ago saying he had been granted leave. But then again, free-spirited Raymond did precisely what Raymond wanted to do, and of the three Rutland sons, he was the least dependable. Mother said it was because he was the middle child.

Theran believed it was simply Raymond's character. He was the only brother who hadn't married, though he'd left a long trail of heartbroken women behind him.

Theran's boot heels clicked on the parquet floor as he traversed the long corridor. The house was blessedly cooler than the outdoors. Was it only two summers ago, the weather had been so cold, the skies so overcast that crops had failed?

After over a week of not knowing if Violetta and Mayven —the tiny baby girl—would survive, mother and daughter gained strength. Though the crisis appeared to be over, and the physician was optimistic, Dr. Parnell would make no promises as yet.

For the first time in a very long while, Theran had actually prayed.

It might not help, but what could it hurt?

Jordan had barely slept or eaten since Theran arrived at Trenthurst House. Theran had offered to take on Jordan's responsibilities so that he could remain with his wife and daughter. Much like himself when in residence at Atherley Hall, Jordan preferred a hands-on approach to managing his estate rather than leaving everything to a steward to manage.

Today, Theran had inspected the dry-stone fence between Jordan's property and Bambrick's. He'd found two places where several stones had tumbled down, which explained why Rutland's banded Galloway cattle had wandered onto their neighbor's property.

A polite note from Poindexter Bambrick yesterday had made them aware of the issue, and men had been sent to retrieve the curious beasts and temporarily repair the wall. A ten-foot stretch of fencing needed repairing.

As Theran lengthened his strides, he cocked his head. Voices filtered from the drawing room, and he puckered his forehead. Still confined to bed, Violetta wasn't entertaining yet, and Mother had made no mention of inviting guests for tea. She wouldn't have done with her daughter-in-law ailing.

A nasty thought unfurled in his mind, and he bit back a vulgar curse.

Surely Albertina Bambrick wouldn't be so crass as to call without an invitation given the crisis in the Rutland household. Devil take her, of course, she would. He'd bet White Flame Athena had accompanied her too.

Theran had never liked nor trusted his stepmother-in-law. The tales Imogene had shared of the woman's pettiness and favoritism toward Athena had left a bad taste in his mouth. For the first few years of her father's marriage to Albertina, Imogene had been at finishing school—at her stepmother's insistence.

Theran was always polite but had never warmed to the woman in the three years he and Imogene had been married, nor in the years since his wife's death.

Unlike her husband, Albertina had made no effort to be

part of Bernadine's life. His daughter scarcely knew her step-grandmother.

Steeling his spine and wrestling his irritation under control, Theran entered the drawing room.

Sure enough, there sat Albertina and Athena in their usual patronizing glory. No other neighbors had been so invasive. The Marquess and Marchioness of Ballister had sent flowers and a consolatory note but hadn't imposed during this trying time.

"Ah, there you are, Theran."

Theran didn't miss the strained lines bracketing his mother's mouth or her lack of reprimand for his tardiness. If anything, she appeared relieved at his arrival.

He crossed to her and kissed her cheek. "Forgive me. My horse threw a shoe, and I had to walk him back to the stables."

Whereas Aunt Melvelia's taste ran to bold and garish, Mother's were far simpler. The drawing room was tastefully decorated in shades of blue, ivory, and gold. No plethora of bric-a-brac adorned every surface, nor was there an abundance of frilly throw pillows.

He'd no sooner finished speaking than Jordan astonished him by ambling in. Purplish crescents still shadowed beneath his eyes, and gaunt hollows accented his cheeks, but he was freshly shaven and wearing clean clothing for the first time in days.

"Darling, I'm so pleased you can join us today." Mother beamed as she poured two more cups of tea. "This is a delicious Darjeeling tea that Raymond sent from India. I think you'll enjoy the light floral flavor."

Ironic that the tea had arrived, but Raymond hadn't.

It was good to see Jordan slowly getting back to normal life. He'd not left Violetta's chamber for more than thirty minutes. His newborn daughter slept in a bassinet in her parents' room because Violetta was terrified to let the tiny infant out of her sight.

Theran accepted his cup and selected the chair farthest from Athena. Hemsworth was right. She did regard Theran like a sweetmeat she wanted to devour.

Or a cat with a cornered mouse.

Athena gave Theran one of her seductress's smiles as he greeted his brother.

"You're looking well, Jord."

Jordan gave him a wry, lopsided grin and accepted his cup from their mother. "Compared to what?"

He sat beside Mother and selected a dainty sandwich which he swallowed in one bite. Another quickly followed. Theran's belly button gnawed at his spine, but he'd chew off his own hand before venturing closer to Athena for a sandwich or biscuit.

"We simply could wait no longer to express sincerest wishes that Violetta and the child make a full recovery." Albertina unfurled her catlike smile while her eyes remained glacial. "They are faring well, yes?"

"Indeed." Mother astutely offered nothing more. She knew when an intrusive fussock was poking her nose into business that wasn't hers.

His mouth full, Jordan merely nodded and selected two more sandwiches.

When was the last time he'd eaten?

"How marvelous." Albertina lifted her teacup to her mouth as she exchanged a gimlet glance with her daughter that suggested otherwise. "We are, of course, delighted at the good news."

Theran rather thought Albertina appeared as if she'd sucked a lemon and was, in fact, here to ascertain if Violetta would live. How his stepmother-in-law ever convinced good-natured Poindexter Bambrick to marry her, Theran couldn't fathom. Kindly, soft-spoken, and seldom annoyed, he'd married a manipulative shrew.

After Imogene's death, Poindexter had wilted into a shadow of his former self. He'd been unwell for some time now. It saddened Theran that his father-in-law's last days wouldn't be spent in comfort and peace. He'd offer to let him live at Atherley Hall, but there was no way Theran would welcome Albertina or Athena into his home.

Through half-lowered eyelids, Theran considered Albertina. Was she truly so gauche that she'd attempt to foist Athena off on another widowed Rutland brother?

Yes. Without hesitation and before the earth had dried over Violetta's grave, he'd vow. She could never fathom that the Rutlands married for love, not convenience, as she had for both of her marriages. Or, to be perfectly candid, for money. Only if the whispers were true, and Theran had reason to believe they were, Bambrick had experienced a reversal in fortunes.

Egads. That was it.

Athena needed to marry well and promptly to prevent her and Albertina from tumbling into financial ruin again.

Why hadn't he discerned Albertina and Athena's game earlier?

Athena's suddenly showing up to *help* with Bernadine. Her resistance to him hiring a governess. Throwing herself at him in Aunt Melvelia's salon. Zounds, he wouldn't have put it past her to crawl into his bed in the middle of the night, then cry foul and force him into marriage.

Purity had saved not only Bernadine that day, but she may very well have spared Theran a horrendous future. Theran had been blinded by grief, but his vision now was perfectly clear.

Athena was a huntress on the prowl for a wealthy

husband, by fair means or foul. And her prey of choice was widowers.

"I planned a small surprise for tea today." Mother slid a troubled glance toward the entrance.

Was she expecting someone else?

Footsteps echoed in the passageway mere moments before Purity entered with the three children. She came to an abrupt halt, her eyes going wide and the color leaching from her face.

Her burgundy gown set off the highlights in her hair and made her skin glow. It also made her eyes sparkle like polished jade. She'd never looked lovelier. He longed to sweep her into his arms and kiss her the way he'd dreamed of doing these past days.

Would she be shocked at his carnal thoughts?

With estimable alacrity, Purity schooled her features into serene composure, but Theran had seen the dread in her eyes. A potent protectiveness rose up in his breast.

He swiftly set his cup aside and rose.

"A splendid surprise indeed, Mother," he said as he crossed to Purity.

"Chin up," he mouthed to her as he took Bernadine's hand. He wished he had the right to put an arm around her shoulder and tell her not to fear. He was there and would ensure no harm came to her.

Purity and Bernadine appeared as if they might dash out the door upon spying Athena.

Lower lip trembling, Bernadine raised doleful green eyes to him.

"It's all right, Rabbit," he murmured. "Papa's here."

A miniature version of Jordan in a navy-blue suit, Jeffery announced, "We're having tea with Grandmama today."

Cheeks yet rounded with baby fat, Landon nodded. "We've been pwacticing ouw mannews with Miss Mayfield."

"Well done, chaps." Jordan motioned for them to join him on the settee. "Come, sit beside me."

Theran expected them to dart to their father's side, but behaving as perfect little gentlemen, they walked toward the ladies and, after executing perfect bows, settled in on either side of their father.

Purity had achieved *that* in a fortnight?

"What an unexpected treat." Albertina didn't spare the children a glance. She trained her entire focus on Purity, a brittle smile nearly cracking her face. "I've not had the pleasure of having tea with my granddaughter yet."

Albertina had never shown the least inclination in being a grandmother to Bernadine.

"Then today is all the more special," Mother skillfully covered. "Albertina, Athena, please permit me to introduce Bernadine's new governess, Miss Purity Mayfield." A smile wreathing her face, Mother set out four more cups and saucers. "Miss Mayfield, these are our neighbors and Theran's in-laws, Mrs. Albertina Bambrick and Miss Athena Sommerville."

"We've met," Athena snapped, her face stamped with haughty outrage. "At the Mumfords' house party."

Teapot raised, Mother glanced up, confused. "Oh?"

"She convinced Theran to send me home, and it appears, has taken my place as governess." Eyes overly bright, and a cunning smile bending her mouth, she delivered the *coup de grâce*. "One doesn't need the second sight to know what means the tart used to persuade him to make *that* bargain."

"Yes," Mrs. Bambrick nodded sagely, malice glinting in her pale blue eyes so much like her daughter's. "The low born will use *anything* at their disposal to achieve their ends."

NINETEEN

Forgive the delay in my reaching Trenthurst House. I met with an unfortunate accident in London and have broken my arm. Once the physician permits me to travel, I shall make straight for home. I have five weeks' leave and look forward to the visit. I have gifts for everyone.

Lt. Raymond Rutland, in a short, sloppy
note penned in his left hand to his mother

Two endlessly long seconds later

"Cherry tarts are my favorite." Bernadine's childish voice rang loudly in the deafening silence that descended on the drawing room. She craned her neck to see the plates of dainties arranged on the tea table. A pout replaced her excitement. "I don't see any tarts."

"*I do,*" Mrs. Bambrick said, spearing Purity with a triumphant glance.

God above.

Mrs. Rutland gasped, her expression aghast.

Jeffery and Landon continued to munch on biscuits, oblivious to the tense undercurrent and foul innuendos.

Theran's and Jordan's black eyebrows crashed together simultaneously, but it was Theran who leveled each woman such a searing glance it was a wonder they didn't go up in ashes on the spot.

"Try a ladyfinger instead, Bernadine." Mrs. Rutland expertly distracted her granddaughter by handing her a biscuit.

Flames of mortification licking scorching paths up her cheeks, Purity wanted to slap the vile women into next Sunday. This was too much. The only reason she didn't verbally fillet them was that children were present.

Flee. Leave. Escape.

"Excuse me."

Purity didn't wait for permission to leave. She turned on her heel and fled. The first scalding tears overflowed onto her cheeks before she made the corridor. God forgive her, but she hated Athena Sommerville and her evil mother for making her cry. Purity was made of sterner stuff. She didn't dissolve into tears over unkind words and despicable insinuations.

"*That* was beyond the pale." Mrs. Rutland's voice crackled with winter frost.

"Purity," Theran called, followed by the unmistakable sound of a teacup dropping and shattering and frustrated male muttering.

"Papa, you broke a cup," Bernadine said.

"I did, love," Theran responded with his typical patience. "It was an accident."

"Jealousy doesn't become you, Miss Sommerville," Jordan intoned with a frigidness to rival his mother's. "Nor does maliciousness you, Mrs. Bambrick. You shall leave my home and never return."

A family feud.

Just what Theran had wanted to avoid.

Mortification cleaved Purity's breast in two, and anger cramped her lungs. Blinded by tears, she stumbled into the passageway and frantically tried to gather her wits. Like a wounded animal, she wanted to hide—to protect herself.

"Come now." Mrs. Bambrick gave an artificial laugh. "You would terminate a friendship of many years over the likes of *her*? She's a nobody. According to Athena, her morals and parentage are questionable."

"*She* has more decency, kindness, and integrity in her little finger than you do in your entire petty, self-centered, and cruel body," Theran grated out.

"Oh my God. I simply cannot credit it." Athena squeaked with such incredulousness that it might've been comical another time. "You...you actually *care* for her. *Her?*"

"I do. Very much, in fact," Theran succinctly agreed. "In the future, I shall only receive Poindexter at Atherley Hall. Neither of you is welcome. Mother, please watch Bernadine for me."

Upon hearing him stride across the drawing room, Purity dashed toward the entrance. She yanked the door open and, not taking the time to shut it, hitched her skirts to her knees and ran as fast as she could down the drive.

Miss Sommerville had vowed to get even. What better way than to destroy Purity's reputation in front of her employer's family?

Never mind that she also maligned Theran with her disgusting allegation.

Purity ran until her lungs burned and her sides ached. Her hair had come free from its pins and swung about her shoulders. Holding her ribs, she bent over, gasping. From the corner of her eye, she caught sight of a small, rustic cottage tucked into the wooded aspen glen.

No smoke rose from the chimney, but it was August, and that didn't mean it was unoccupied. She prayed it might be and also that it would be unlocked. She could take respite inside for a while. Not only was she chagrined at being accused of prostituting herself, but she'd also lost her head and ran away, which only made her look guilty.

"Purity? Purity?" Theran pursued her. "Purity, where are you? Let's talk. Please."

Purity couldn't face him just yet. By no means was any of this Theran's fault. He was as much a victim as she. Yet it stung to be called a whore, that anyone would suggest she'd only attained the governess position by prostituting herself.

Purity had more pride than she'd realized and was capable of more rage than she wanted to acknowledge. In truth, she wished Athena Sommerville and Albertina Bambrick a swift journey to the lowest level of hell for besmirching her character.

In time, she *might* forgive them.

With a frantic glance around, she dashed toward the cottage.

The handle gave way with one push, and she shoved the door open.

"Hello?"

Venturing inside, she called again. "Hello? Is anyone here?"

Only silence greeted her.

Relief washed over her, and she swiftly shut the door.

Rotating slowly, she inspected the deserted cottage. A stone fireplace, before which sat a dilapidated velvet wingback chair and a ratty footstool, took up most of the opposite wall. A cabinet and a humble table with two chairs occupied another beneath a window. A door led to another room on the last wall where several pegs protruded over low shelves. A bedchamber, she supposed.

Cobwebs clung to the ceiling corners and several of the fireplace's stones. Her shoes stirring up dust on the floor, she advanced farther into the small space. She sneezed, then sneezed again. Withdrawing a clean handkerchief from her right pocket, she wiped her damp face and blew her nose before tucking it into her left pocket.

With a sigh, she sank onto the worn wingback chair.

Once again, she'd taken the coward's way.

You...you care for her.

I do. Very much, in fact.

Theran cared for Purity.

But only as his daughter's governess—possibly former governess now. Purity wasn't foolish enough to read more into his words. Even if in her heart, he'd secretly come to mean something more to her over these past weeks.

How could she have done the unthinkable?

Come to care for Theran?

To love him?

Hadn't Mrs. Shepherd warned all of her pupils against that very thing?

Perhaps lessons and exercises on guarding one's heart and emotions ought to be taught at Haven House and Academy for the Enrichment of Young Women.

Purity shook her head and cringed.

What must Mrs. Rutland and Theran's brother think?

From their responses, they'd been outraged at Miss Sommerville's and her mother's behavior. That, unfortunately, didn't mean they might not give some credence to the accusations. What was more, the accusations had been made in front of children.

Had those harpies no bounds?

Closing her eyes, she rested her head against the chair's tall back. Hiding like a child was immature. She'd have to return and face everyone—hold her head high while she waited to learn her fate. Theran knew Miss Sommerville lied, but could he convince his family?

At least she had Lady Ceddes's letter of reference, and Chasity said she'd recommend her for a position at Balderbrook's Institution for Genteel Ladies.

God would provide.

Yes, He always had.

Nonetheless, if Purity was forced to move on, her heart would remain behind with the darling little girl she was fast coming to love as her own—and Bernadine's father, whom she had come to love even though it was wrong and she should've known better.

TWENTY

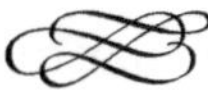

*I've only just learned that Balderbrook's Institution for
Genteel Ladies has restructured the London school, and
only one instructor position remains. If you are interested
in applying, I urge you to do so at your earliest convenience.
I know your tenure with the Ceddes is at an end soon.
My invitation to stay with me is always open too.*

~Chasity Terramier, in a short note
to Purity Mayfield

Gamekeeper's Cottage
Trenthurst House Estate
A short while later

Theran caught a flash of crimson between the alder trees.
    Purity.
    Why had she run from him?
    Hadn't he promised that he wouldn't let anything happen

to her? That he'd protect her? Even from despicable false accusations? From vindictive women bent on her downfall?

Mayhap she hadn't believed him.

He slowed his pace, realizing Purity had spotted the abandoned gamekeeper's cottage. It hadn't been used for at least twenty years.

Purity had never had anyone to champion her before. Had always had to rely on herself.

Not anymore. She had him now—would always have him if he could persuade her to marry him.

He laughed, the unfettered laughter of pure joy.

He loved Purity with a love that defied human definition.

That very first day, when his eyes met hers for the first time, his soul had recognized what it had taken his mind much longer to acknowledge.

Theran had loved Imogene. Very much. She'd been his first love. Theran hadn't believed he could ever love so profoundly again. But despite his anger toward the Almighty and that he didn't deserve it, God had granted him a deep, pure, abiding love.

It was a glorious sensation that rejuvenated his soul, invigorated his spirit, and gave him hope for his future. A future with Purity and Bernadine. Hopefully, a future with more children.

Theran pressed the latch and entered the shadowy cottage. It must be close to half-past five, and with the trees shading it, little sunlight filtered into the building. It took a moment for his eyes to adjust to the dim interior.

"Purity?"

A slight movement near the fireplace drew his attention.

She looked around the side of the chair, her magnificent hair framing her face and looking so vulnerable, his heart ached for her. "I just needed a little time by myself." Her gaze sank to her hand resting on the chair's arm. "I'm sorry, Theran."

In an instant, he was before her. Dropping to a knee, Theran cradled her cheek in his palm. "You've absolutely nothing to be sorry for. Nothing."

She'd been crying. Pools of fern-green framed by spiky, sooty lashes peered back at him.

"I should have stayed—braved it out." She glanced away for a moment. "I never thought of myself as a coward, but when they said..."

"Shh, darling." Theran kissed her temple as if it were the most natural thing in the world. "You and I know it's not true. That's what matters."

"Your family..." She pushed her hair over her shoulder.

"Will believe what I tell them. Besides, my mother and brother know Athena's and Albertina's characters well. They were perpetually unkind to my wife."

Purity searched his eyes, hers soft at the edges with unnamed emotion. "We should go back. The children..."

"They are well taken care of." It was Theran's turn to hesitate. "Purity...?"

What if she didn't feel the same way?

Other than the time he'd almost kissed her after Ceddes' attack, he'd never hinted at his budding feelings. He'd presumed it was too soon. But now...Theran didn't know how he'd keep from telling her how she'd enchanted him. Had stolen bits and pieces of his heart until he'd not been able to keep from falling in love with her.

Well, there was no rush.

He could be patient.

Theran would simply woo her and, in time, convince Purity to marry him.

Lips slightly parted, Purity angled her head. "Yes?"

He dropped his focus to her mouth, and as if sensing his intent, her tongue darted out and dampened the plump pillows.

"I'm going to kiss you," he whispered when his mouth was a fraction from hers.

"You are?"

"I am. If you allow it."

"I...I do."

Grazing his mouth over hers, Theran tasted the velvety, honeyed sweetness of her lips.

"I've wanted to do this for some time," he confessed with a boyish grin.

Dawning understanding lit her eyes, and his heart took on an irregular beat at the joy shining there. "You have?"

"I have, and it has taken a great deal of restraint on my part not to yield to my desire." He rested his forehead against hers.

"I didn't know." She shyly touched his face. "I've wanted you to kiss me."

Dropping to both knees, Theran wrapped his arms around Purity and pulled her to his chest. This time when his mouth met hers, the hunger, the passion, and the love he'd kept tamped down surged to the surface. He kissed her like a drowning man, and only Purity could save his life. His soul.

She wriggled until she was on her knees upon the chair and wound her arms around his back.

The kiss went on and on and on.

Each sigh, each caress, each sliding of lips against the other's, was an intoxicating dance.

Purity kissed him back, her inexperience endearing and electrifying. Her little moans and sighs drove Theran to the brink of self-control.

He must stop. He'd been too long without a woman, and he would not take Purity outside the bonds of matrimony.

With a great deal of reluctance, he lifted his head.

"We should return to the house," he said. "I'm sure Mother and Jordan are worried about you."

Nodding, Purity stood and shook out her skirts. "Yes. I don't wish them to fret. Especially the children."

She was always so considerate of others.

Theran would not propose to Purity here in this dingy cottage. When he asked this marvelous woman to marry him, he'd do it properly. Romantically with a ring, pretty words, and in a setting where spiders weren't witnesses.

Please, God. Let her say yes.

TWENTY ONE

As promised, I have forwarded your trunk and the correspondence Lady Ceddes had delivered to Mottford Hall. I regret we never had the opportunity to have that private chat. Perhaps another opportunity will arise to do so. I am confident you are managing exceptionally well in your position as Bernadine's governess.

~Melvelia Hawtrey, Countess of Mumford,
in a brief missive to
Miss Purity Mayfield

Trenthurst House Gardens
Mid-morning
8 September 1818

As had become the pattern these past two weeks, Purity had incorporated a lesson in the children's exploration of the gardens. Today, they were on the hunt for insects. As the brothers and their cousin scoured the flowers and bushes for crawlies, she reflected on her return to the house early yesterday evening.

Mrs. Rutland had declared Purity should take the evening off from her duties. Theran had readily agreed. His brother, dutiful as always, had already returned to his wife's bedside.

Such love and commitment warmed Purity's heart. It also made her long for such a relationship—something she'd not done before meeting Theran. Pragmatism had always guided her decisions and actions. Until a moppet with fiery hair had entered her life, introducing her to the only man to make her lose her temper and long for a life other than the one her heritage destined for her.

A lovely scented bath had been prepared for her, and a dinner tray with a scrumptious, flaky chicken pie, fruit, cheese, and utterly decadent lemon cream for dessert had been delivered a short while later. Purity had meant to read for a while and then bid the children goodnight, but sleep had overtaken her, and she'd not awoken until six this morning.

She'd leaped from the bed and dashed about to complete her morning ablutions.

Purity's mouth yet tingled from Theran's kisses.

Naturally, at eight and twenty, she'd imagined what it would be like to be kissed. However, the experience had proved more exquisite, more enthralling, than she ever could've dreamed.

She'd fallen in love with Theran.

The very thing a governess was warned to never, ever do. At least her employer wasn't married.

Giggles carried to her as the Rutland boys chased each other back and forth around the pristinely tended garden.

Bernadine, rather than search for bugs, sniffed blossoms here and there.

Scrunching her forehead, Purity tried to decipher exactly what had happened in the gamekeeper's cottage—what it meant, if anything. Theran had said he'd dreamed of kissing her for some time.

Surely that meant he held her in some regard.

Didn't it?

She and Theran had walked in silence back to the house hand in hand until they were close enough that someone might see them. He'd taken a different door inside to avoid speculation and tattle.

Given Mrs. Rutland and Jordan's warm reception at breakfast, Purity laid aside her fears from yesterday of censure and termination. She bent to smell a luscious yellow rose. Soon autumn would descend upon the countryside, and the garden's beauty would fade until spring.

Purity wasn't sure how much longer they'd remain at Trenthurst House, but until they left, she'd continue helping with Jeffery and Landon.

Jeffery jumped off a bench then squatted to examine the small, colorful rocks covering the footpath.

"Jeffery, what do we know about insects?"

He grinned, revealing a missing front tooth. "They have six legs."

"Excellent." Purity lifted a ladybird from a rose leaf. It crawled up her finger. "What else do we know about insects, Landon?"

He held a stick out like a fencing sword. "Umm..."

"How do they fly?" she asked, coaching him.

"Wings. They have wings," he announced proudly as he wielded his make-believe weapon.

"They do, indeed," she agreed. "Bernadine? Do you know anything about insects?

Bernadine wrinkled her nose. "They are icky."

The boys burst into giggles.

"Look, I have a ladybird beetle." Purity held out her hand. "Let's count her spots, shall we?"

The children rushed over.

"Miss Mayfield?"

Purity glanced over her shoulder to where Karen, one of the Rutlands' friendly maids, stood in the doorway.

"A trunk and several correspondences have arrived for you," Karen said with a cheery smile. "They have been put in your room. Mrs. Rutland thought perhaps you wished to read the letters. I shall take the children to the kitchen while you do. Cook just took gingerbread from the oven and said they might have a piece."

That brought cheers from the three, and they rushed to Karen's side then disappeared through the french window before Purity could thank her.

Purity gently brushed the ladybird beetle onto a leaf. After a final glance around the peaceful garden, she made her way to her chamber. A neat stack of letters, tied together with a blue ribbon, lay upon the rosewood night table.

Purity removed her bonnet, set it upon her bed's light blue counterpane, and untied the scrap of ribbon.

On the top was a note from Trinity Ablethorne. Beneath it was a missive from Lady Mumford, another from Chasity Terramier, one from Mercy Brockman, and on the bottom of the short stack was a letter from Mrs. Hester Shepherd.

Sitting upon her bed, Purity skimmed over her friends' letters. Trinity said she understood Purity's hasty departure and that they'd catch up later. Chasity wanted to let Purity know that Balderbrook's Institution for Genteel Ladies only had one position left.

Purity smiled and set the letter aside.

She wouldn't be applying. For the time being, she was perfectly content to remain Bernadine's governess.

Mercy had invited her for a Christmastide house party. Joy, Faith, and the others were also invited. Purity would like to attend, but would Theran permit it?

Probably.

He was nothing like the Ceddes.

Curious as to why Mrs. Shepherd had written, Purity cracked the seal. A few moments later, she gasped and clapped a hand to her mouth.

It couldn't be true.

Heart racing and her stomach knotted, she reread the letter three times.

Dropping her hand holding the letter onto her lap, Purity stared blindly across the room.

A bevy of emotions assaulted her one right after the other: Disbelief. Joy. Anger. Exhilaration. Wonderment. Excitement. Confusion. Incredulousness. And finally, sorrow.

Her focus sank to the perfectly formed script lining the foolscap. Purity had an uncle, and not only had he been named her guardian by her father, but he was also a marquess. The Marquess of Ballister.

Theran's neighbor.

This changed everything.

Did she want things to change?

I don't know.

She loved Theran and Bernadine. How could she leave them? But Theran had made no mention of honorable intent after their kiss.

What if...?

Her mind shied away from the awful thought, but Purity forced herself to finish it. To face what might be the truth.

What if Theran only toyed with her affections?

Or had given into a moment's lust?

With an almost hysterical laugh, Purity shook her head.

A soft knock at the door shook her from her reverie.

In a haze of shock and incredulity, she stood and crossed the room on shaky legs, still holding the letter. Filling her lungs with a bracing breath, she did what she had done for so many years and arranged her features into a tranquil, benign expression.

She opened the door.

Theran stood there, a shadow of concern sharpening the planes and angles of his face. His deep-blue coat was a near match for his midnight-blue eyes. Those eyes. Every time she glanced into them, she was lost.

He hadn't been at breakfast. He tipped his mouth into one of his devastating smiles, and her whole body threatened to melt.

"I wanted to speak to you this morning, Purity, but there was an incident I had to attend to on Jordan's behalf." He scratched behind his ear. "You have a caller. Mother sent me up to fetch you."

She jerked her head up, searching his eyes. "*I* have a caller?"

"You do." He reverently touched her cheek with a bent finger. "Promise we'll speak afterward, Purity. That you won't make any decisions until we talk."

A mixture of intensity and tenderness etched his dear features.

"All right, I promise." How could she deny him anything?

"Is everything all right? You are pale." Theran's attention sank to the letter she still clutched before slowly lifting.

Wordlessly, she handed over the letter. Soon, everyone would know the contents in any event.

Her stomach churning, she folded her arms across her middle and waited for him to read it. When he finished, he refolded the letter with a serious expression and lifted the paper in the air.

"He's below, Purity. Your uncle, the Marquess of Ballister, is below."

TWENTY TWO

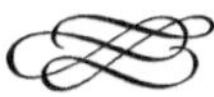

You cannot imagine my relief in knowing Violetta and the babe are recovering. I would've come to offer my assistance if I didn't have a house full of guests. Once they depart, Herbert and I shall waste no time in journeying to Trenthurst House.

Please advise Theran for me that the puppy he selected for Bernadine will be ready to leave her mother, and we will bring the pup for Bernadine's birthday present.

~Melvelia Hawtrey, Countess of Mumford,
in a letter to her sister,
Mrs. Celena Rutland

Trenthurst House Drawing Room
Five Minutes Later

Theran remained with Purity as she made her way to the drawing room, instinctively understanding she needed him for support. Yesterday, she'd been viciously slandered, and today, she had discovered she wasn't alone in the world. That in fact, she was niece to a wealthy and powerful peer.

A part of Theran was terrified she'd pack her belongings today and embrace the incredible opportunity fate had given her. Another part of him rejoiced that her uncle had found her.

He also cursed himself as ten kinds of a fool for not declaring himself in the gamekeeper's cottage. At least then, Purity would know he loved her and wanted to make her his wife.

What must she think of him?

Of what had transpired between them?

As they neared the drawing room, she gave him a weak smile and squared her shoulders. "Into the den of lions."

Brave darling.

"Not a bit of it. Ballister is a splendid chap. Honorable, kind, a faithful husband and loving father."

She chuckled and shook her head. "I was jesting, Theran."

Grasping her hand, he lifted it to his mouth and pressed a fervent kiss on her fingertips.

He must tell her. Now.

"Now may not be the time, and God knows it's not the place. Nor is this how I would've chosen to tell you." Theran glanced at the closed door. "But I want you to know before we go inside that I love you, Purity."

Crystal tears glistened in her eyes, and she opened her mouth.

He put a finger to her lips.

"Not now. Don't say anything now." He kissed her forehead, breathing in her essence. "Wait until you hear what your uncle has to say."

After a long moment, she gave a shallow nod.

He knocked on the door and ushered her in when Jordan bid them enter.

Purity paused a few steps in the drawing room.

Paul Beckwith, the Marquess of Ballister, and his younger brother, Toliver, sat in armchairs adjacent to the pair of settees. His wife, Ellise, and Toliver's wife, Therese, shared one settee while Mother occupied her usual place on the other. Jordan stood beside the unlit fireplace.

All trained their gazes on Purity.

At her entrance, her uncles rose.

"My word, she looks just like Marie," Therese Beckwith exclaimed, resplendent in what was no doubt the latest Paris fashion. She clutched Ellise's hand. "Marie was your mother," she added by way of explanation.

Theran had thought Purity looked familiar too, and now that she was in the same room as her uncles, he understood why. There was a distinct family resemblance—mainly the eye and hair color.

Paul came forward, his hands outstretched, a wide smile arching his mouth. "Purity. Words cannot express how delighted I am that we are finally meeting."

He gave her a peck on the cheek.

Toliver did the same. "We were astonished and so happy to recently learn you'd survived the fire."

Appearing rather dazed, Purity managed a tremulous smile.

"Purity, have a seat beside me." Mother patted the settee, and Purity offered a grateful upward sweep of her mouth.

Theran went to stand beside his brother, who gave him a searching look. Jordan had always been able to read Theran. He probably already knew Theran was heads over tail for Purity.

Paul and Toliver resumed their seats.

"To think, we have had a detective searching all of England for you, and here you are, right next door," Therese said.

"I wrote you a few weeks ago. Sent the letter to Petherwick Court." Paul leaned forward. "Didn't you receive my letter?"

Purity accepted the cup of tea Mother offered her. "I'm afraid not, my lord."

"None of that." He waved a hand. "You must call me Uncle Paul."

"Absolutely," Toliver agreed, beaming. "We don't stand on formality in this family."

"I recently changed employers, and I can only assume your letter was lost in the forwarding." Purity took a sip of tea.

Theran would wager that bugger Ceddes had something to do with the letter's disappearance.

"Ah," Paul said. "Well, as I explained in the letter, your father, Clarence, named me your guardian. He was two years younger than me and a year older than Toliver." Paul took a drink of his tea. "Your parents died in a fire, but your nurse managed to get you out. She took you to our father."

His features folded into a disgusted expression.

"Our father never approved of Clarence marrying a commoner," Toliver put in. "We have surmised he sent you to the foundling home where you were raised and told us you'd perished as well."

"How did you find me?" Purity asked.

Paul scratched his forehead. "When I came into the title a few months ago, my man of affairs and I were inspecting the ledgers. We noticed annual payments to Haven House and Academy for the Enrichment of Young beginning shortly after the fire. They continued for several years. I became suspicious and hired an investigator."

"Who contacted Mrs. Shepherd." Purity set her cup down

with only the merest rattle. A wan half-smile curved her mouth. "I only just read Mrs. Shepherd's letter today."

Paul lifted a shoulder. "So you are aware of the inquiry and her participation, though she was ignorant of my father's nefarious scheme."

"Yes." Purity looked at each of her uncles and aunts in turn. "It is a lot to take in."

"We would like to invite you to tea tomorrow, Purity," her Aunt Ellise said, then puzzled her brow. "Or would you prefer to be called Caroline now? That is your given name. Caroline Aimee Beckwith."

No, she's Purity.

Purity shook her head. "I've been Purity for as long as I can recall."

"Very good," Paul said. "Purity it is then."

"As Ellise was saying, we'd love for you to come to tea tomorrow and meet your cousins." Therese's eyes twinkled. "You have nine. Toliver and I have five children, and Paul and Ellise four. They range in age from fifteen to three and thirty."

"I should like that." Purity relaxed against the settee and offered her first genuine smile. "Very much."

"Celena, you, Theran, and Jordan are invited as well," Ellise said. "I know that Violetta is still recovering else, naturally, we'd include her."

"I thank you," Jordan said. "But until Violetta is healthier, I'm not accepting any invitations."

"Understandable," Therese murmured.

"We've already prepared a room for you." Ellise brushed a crumb from her mazarine-blue gown. "You can move in at your earliest convenience. I am quite looking forward to it as my daughter married last spring."

Purity shot a panicked glance to Theran.

"Ellise." Paul shook his head. "Not now, dearest. We can discuss all of the details later."

Oh, bugger it.

Theran wasn't waiting to propose.

Clearing his throat, he stepped forward. Bending his neck, he cupped his nape and fashioned a sheepish grin. "I'm afraid I may well put a damper in your plans, Paul."

Frowning, Paul canted his head. "How so?"

"I intended to propose to Purity today," Theran said, his gaze locked with hers.

The women gasped.

"Marvelous." Grinning like a Cheshire cat, Mother clapped. "Splendid. Absolutely splendid."

"I knew it." Jordan chuckled, slapping Theran on the back. "I knew it. Even told Violetta."

In three strides, Theran was in front of Purity. Pride be hanged. He'd propose and pray she accepted. Her emotional response in the corridor had sent his heart to singing and given him the hope and courage he needed.

He sank onto one knee and took her hand.

"How romantic," Therese whispered.

"I love you, Purity. So much, in truth, that it frightens me but also makes me deliriously happy."

Fully aware every eye in the room regarded him with rapt attention, Theran cupped her face tenderly between his hands.

"I want you to be Bernadine's mother and for us to have children together. You brought me back to life, and I long to marry you more than anything in the world. I want to spend the rest of my days loving you. Please, tell me you love me too and that you'll marry me?"

Purity swept her gaze over the others before bringing it back to settle on Theran.

Only the *tick-tock, tick-tock, tick-tock* of the long case clock interrupted the pregnant silence.

Holding his breath, Theran sent up a silent prayer.

Forgive me, God, for doubting you. I don't understand all of your ways, but please, please, let her say yes.

"I love you too." An adorable blush turned Purity's cheeks pink. "I'll marry you."

The room exploded in applause, and cries of congratulations rang loudly.

It was scandalous, simply not done in polite circles, but right there in front of everyone, Theran sealed their troth with a thorough kiss.

She was his one. His only. His lady.

EPILOGUE

I know it's short notice, but Theran and I are to be married October first at my uncle, the Marquess of Ballister's home. It would mean so much if you could be there.

I shall explain then how my uncle found me.

~Miss Purity Mayfield, in a wedding
invitation to her closest friends,
Joy Morrisette, Mercy Brockman,
Chasity Terramier, Faith Roth, and
Trinity Ablethorne

Brightwicke Park
Home of the Marquess and Marchioness of Ballister
4 October 1818 – Early Afternoon

Her family.

Pausing at the entrance to her aunt and uncle's drawing room, Purity's heart overflowed with love and thankfulness. When she was an old, old woman, she would cherish the memory of the tableau before her.

Violetta, holding a sleeping Mayven, sat beside Jordan as they chatted with Lord and Lady Mumford. Chasity and Aston, Mercy and Ronan, and Joy and Brandon burst into laughter at something Raymond Rutland said. He'd arrived three weeks ago with his arm in a splint, which he still wore.

He was every bit the charming rogue Theran said he was.

Uncle Paul and Uncle Toliver were arguing good-naturedly over a proposed bill in Parliament. Their wives exchanged knowing glances. Purity had learned her uncles frequently debated each other on political matters.

Her cousins, and their spouses and children, had come for her and Theran's wedding and stayed to celebrate Bernadine's birthday. Outside, Jeffery, Landon, and Bernadine played with the other children and the new puppy—appropriately named Dotty.

"Happy, Mrs. Rutland?" Theran approached from behind and wrapped his arms around her waist.

She put her hands atop his folded over her abdomen where perhaps already a babe had begun to grow. "Um-hum. Deliriously so."

"Me too. I thank God every day for answering my prayer."

"Mine too." Tears of happiness pricked behind her eyelids. She slanted her neck to look up at him. "I thought you didn't put much stock in religious falderol," she teased.

"Forgive me for that, darling. Those words were spoken from a place of wounding."

"I know, and I forgave you long ago."

He quirked a rakish black eyebrow. "You look quite fetching in that gown. Another borrowed from your cousin?"

Purity glanced down at the seafoam green gown her cousin Laura had given her. "A gift from Laura. She said it was last Season's. It's the loveliest gown I've ever worn."

Theran rested his chin on her head.

"I must go to London in a fortnight. I wish for you and Bernadine to come along. I intend to purchase you an entirely new wardrobe, down to new frilly underthings." The last he uttered in a naughty whisper.

"Theran!" Purity cast a scandalized glance around. "Hush. Someone will overhear you."

"We are newlyweds." He tilted her head so her eyes met his. "They will understand."

Poindexter Bambrick excused himself from a discussion with Purity's cousins Roger and Michael and made his way to them.

A gentle, humble man in the middle of his sixth decade, Poindexter appeared far older. His marriage to Albertina had aged him.

"I appreciate you inviting me to Bernadine's birthday celebration."

"Of course, Dexter," Theran said, coming around to Purity's side. "We are family."

Dexter removed his spectacles and wiped them with his handkerchief. "Yes, indeed. Now that Albertina has gone to live with Athena and her husband, I hope to be able to visit my granddaughter more often."

He looked rather like a starving dog eager for a bone or a scrap of food tossed his way.

Athena had finally snared a husband—a much, *much* older husband. Wealthy too. No surprise they'd been caught in a compromising situation by Albertina and two of her most gossipy cronies a mere week after Jordan had ordered the two women from his house.

Theran put his arm around Dexter's frail shoulders. "I can do much better than that, Dexter. Purity and I would count ourselves fortunate if you agreed to live with us."

Tears blurred Dexter's eyes as he shifted his gaze from Theran to Purity.

"You wouldn't mind, Purity? It wouldn't bother you that Imogene was my daughter?"

Purity stepped forward and kissed his wrinkled cheek. "You are my family now."

Theran winked. "You see why I fell in love with her?"

Chuckling and drying his eyes, Dexter nodded. "I do, my boy. I do, indeed."

Bernadine came running into the drawing room, Dotty scrambling to keep up behind her.

"Grandpa!"

Arms open wide, she hurled herself at Dexter.

Her grandfather kissed her flushed cheek.

Theran scooped the wriggling puppy into his arms.

"I told you, Papa." Grinning, Bernadine petted her puppy.

Dotty promptly tried to nibble her fingers, and Bernadine laughed.

"Told me what, Rabbit?" The puppy bit his chin. "Stop that, you little rascal."

"That Purty should be my mama."

His gaze suspiciously moist again, Dexter said, "Out of the mouth of babes."

"You were absolutely right." Theran's gaze met Purity's, and he leaned over and grazed his lips across hers.

Yes, Purity thought as she let her eyelashes drift shut. *This is absolutely right.*

If you'd like to leave a review, I would be grateful.

Keep reading for a free preview of
NEVER A PROPER LADY
Secrets of Scandalous Ladies, Book Five

NEVER A PROPER LADY
Secrets of Scandalous Ladies
Book 5

Naturally, I shall attend Lottie's wedding, but I cannot promise to remain for the house party's duration. You know how much I detest the boorish things, Edie. Particularly as I know our odious Kellinggrave cousins will be present.

Besides, my research won't permit me to fritter away an entire week on frivolous activities. Toward that end, my amanuensis, my valet, and perhaps even my research assistant shall accompany me to Dovetonwick Court.

Please inform Mother and ask her to make the arrangements. Also, give her, Lottie, and the rest my warmest regards. Expect us Thursday next.

~Lord Constantine Kellinggrave, in
response to his sister,
Lady Edyth Kellinggrave's
reminder of their sister's upcoming nuptials

29 August 1818
Bedford Square, London, England
A few minutes past seven in the morning

Shirtsleeves rolled to his elbows and sans jacket and waistcoat, Constantine—Con to his closest friends and family—stood before his scuffed and scarred double-sided walnut partner desk. Eyes narrowed, he cocked his head, listening.

Yes, the brisk footsteps he'd come to recognize these past few days announced his amanuensis had arrived for work. Early again, as she had been every day since he'd grudgingly retained her services.

Regrettably, he couldn't fault her for her promptness.

Time to don his armor, gird his loins, gather his shield and sword, and prepare for battle.

He swept a gaze around the room, which had become less research sanctuary and more combat zone in recent days.

Soft rays of sunshine filtered through the open navy-blue draperies festooning the three arched windows opposite the long room. The streams of sunlight caressed the equally scuffed and scarred oak floor and the single taupe, crimson, and cerulean-blue Aubusson carpet sprawled haphazardly in the center of the rectangular room.

Dust motes floated in the luminous beams, performing a taunting dance before they drifted to rest on the myriad of surfaces cluttered with specimens, journals, documents, and all manner of curiosities. And dust. A fine layer coated almost everything.

Gilly, the once emaciated mongrel of undeterminable pedigree Constantine had rescued from the streets two years ago, lay prone upon the floor, soaking in those same rays. As if sensing his master's focus, Gilly thumped his wiry, multi-colored tail once without deigning to open his copper-brown eyes.

A wry grin pulled Constantine's mouth upward on one side.

Gilly had taken to a life of luxury and ease as readily as a nobly born duke.

The feminine stride grew closer and, if possible, even sharper, as if the deceptively decorous Miss Faith Roth announced with her dainty feet what she didn't dare say with her pink Cupid's bow mouth.

Not that he initially noticed her pretty mouth.

It's just that she so often pursed those plump lips, pulled them into a disapproving ribbon, or bit the lower pillow—no doubt to prevent telling him to bugger himself—that he couldn't help but notice how nicely shaped they were.

Never mind Miss Roth's lips.

Another day of subtle verbal sparring and intellectual dueling was about to commence.

You enjoy matching wits with her.

Constantine snorted, and Gilly cracked open a sleepy eye.

Determining naught was amiss, the dog relaxed and resumed his nap with a shuddery sigh.

Not by half, Constantine didn't enjoy the daily scuffles with his scribe. No more than he'd relish a carbuncle on his bum or appreciate a monstrous stye in his eye.

Refusing to look toward the entrance, yet acutely aware of each clipped step drawing Miss Faith Roth nearer, he drew his eyebrows together as he considered the scientific journals he held in either hand.

Would he have time to read either or both while traveling to Dovetonwick Court for his sister's wedding? Likely. With a nonchalant shrug, he added the books to the stack of papers, books, and documents he'd already placed inside his satchel.

Naturally, not attending the nuptials wasn't an option—Mother would never forgive Constantine—and he wanted to see Lottie exchange her vows.

Regardless, this was a deuced inconvenient time to leave his research.

In truth, there was never a good time for a man who preferred scientific studies to socializing with vain, self-important denizens. Many of whom looked down their aristocratic noses at his *hobby*. But as the third son of Harland Kellinggrave, Duke of Landrith, they daren't overtly disdain Constantine or the work he took seriously.

Pompous hypocrites.

Moreover, a fortnight ago, his faithful and reliable research assistant, Harvey Camberg-Trainer, had fallen in love with the pretty clerk at the new French patisserie and boulangerie. Now Harvey was distracted more often than not and had actually confused a Holly Blue butterfly with a common blue just yesterday.

Harvey's doleful countenance and soul-rending sighs every few minutes as he rested his chin upon his fist and gazed forlornly out the window were enough to cause Constantine to clench his teeth and swear beneath his breath.

Must love render men bacon-brained sots?

Buffleheaded idiots?

Constantine had never suffered from the affliction—praise

the saints—but two of his closest chums had. Half the time, he scarcely recognized the perpetually grinning dolts anymore.

If Harvey brought another bag of pastries or loaf of bread to work, Mrs. Mettlebank might well give her notice. The cook didn't appreciate another outshining her culinary talents. Even Constantine had to admit the French baked goods were superior to anything Mrs. Mettlebank had ever served.

He'd bite his tongue off before admitting that fact, however.

Mrs. Mettlebank accepted his idiosyncrasies, including that he rarely dined on any type of schedule. And she didn't grumble about him wandering into the kitchen at all hours for a snack. More often than not, she left a plate of something or other for him to sample.

More irksome than Harvey's infatuation, however, was Faith Roth, the scrivener Constantine had recently hired. And who, any second now, would march into the laboratory-office and, with a single astute glance from those chocolatey doe eyes behind her wire-rimmed spectacles, under sardonically arched strawberry blonde eyebrows, would prick his temper.

As surely and as deliberately as if she'd poked him with a needle.

Had a more exasperating woman ever walked the earth?

She seemed particularly fond of sending verbal darts in his direction, always with a benign expression and perfectly respectable tone.

Miss Faith Roth didn't fool him for a second.

Beneath her cool and calm exterior bubbled molten lava. Unless he missed his guess—and he was positive he did not— she'd erupt someday, and anyone nearby would get scorched.

Despite her outward poise and decorum, Miss Roth had become a proverbial thorn in Constantine's side. He'd yet to see her lose her temper, but her expressive eyes rung him a peal at least half a dozen times daily.

He couldn't terminate her either because not only was she efficient, organized, and an excellent scribe—which Constantine admitted he badly needed—he'd only hired her because he'd lost a bet.

A silly, thoughtless wager he never ought to have placed and wouldn't have done so if he hadn't had one brandy too many, and if Lord Ronan Brockman and Aston Terramier hadn't accused him of being archaic in his beliefs and resistant to social progress—specifically when it came to women.

Those two disgustingly in love chaps thought it hysterical that Constantine had hired Faith Roth, who just happened to be—God save him—bosom friends with their sweethearts.

Fate had an irregular sense of humor.

By Jove, Lord Constantine Peyton Harland Kellinggrave was *not* antiquated in his thinking.

Despite ridicule and condescension, wasn't he going beyond the bounds and researching the effects of butterflies and moths on pollination?

Pollination was crucial for crops, orchards, and even kitchen gardens. Bees generally received all of the attention, but moths and butterflies traveled greater distances and contributed mightily to pollination as well.

He tapped his chin with his forefinger.

Hmm. Were nectar-feeding bats also pollinators?

That might be interesting to study as well, but first things first.

Miss Faith Roth.

The perpetual pebble in his shoe. The burr on his bum. The itch he couldn't reach.

If Constantine gave his scrivener her *congé* before six months passed, he'd have to admit defeat and pay the wager. It wasn't losing the funds that made him reluctant. It was that he'd have to admit there might be a measure of truth—surely, only the merest amount—in his friends' accusation.

Why was a young woman of excellent character so set on proving herself in a traditionally male occupation? Not that females couldn't perform the task just as well, but the women he knew focused their energies on marriage and having children.

The gentlemanliness bred into Constantine's very core as an aristocrat also objected to the dishonor of hiring her purely to win a wager. That had been the craven act of a cad, and he felt no small amount of shame for his role in the fiasco.

That Miss Roth had overheard him arguing with Harvey about why he'd hired her only added to Constantine's guilt. Now, every time Miss Roth glanced in his direction, he felt miniature accusatory daggers pricking him.

Grunting, he plunked his hands on his hips and perused his disorderly research laboratory and office once more. Which was, in fact, the entire ground floor of his house except for the kitchen.

How hard would it be to convince Miss Roth to accompany him to Dovetonwick Court? He had mentioned possible travel as part of her duties during the farcical interview, hoping the duty would dissuade her from accepting the post. It hadn't.

Confounded woman.

If Constantine dictated to her during the journey, that would make up for the time lost participating in obligatory family activities.

He wished to depart for Dovetonwick Court on Tuesday —three days away.

"Good morning, my lord."

Formal, cool, civil.

Constantine painted a pleasant expression on his face and summoned a welcoming smile.

"Good morning, Miss Roth. I trust you slept well."

He barely constrained the grin tipping his lips upward at her swift, suspicious glance. He'd never bothered to inquire about her sleep or any other personal details, for that matter, before.

Except for the perfunctory questions he'd asked during their initial meeting, he knew nothing about her. Beyond her name, age—three and twenty—education, that she was an orphan, and that her letters of reference were exceptional.

Of course, the latter could've been forged, but he believed them genuine.

Of the three women who'd answered his advert, Miss Roth was the candidate he'd erroneously believed would quit within a week.

More fool him.

Everything he'd done to encourage Miss Roth's departure had only caused her to dig her heels and claws in and thwart his efforts all the more. Always within the bounds of respectfulness and deference.

Only just.

Gilly leaped to his feet and trotted over to Miss Roth, wagging his tail with such exuberance that his entire back end wiggled.

Traitor.

"Good morning to you too, handsome boy," Miss Roth crooned, bending to give the dog a pat and kiss, and presenting her delightfully rounded derriere for leisurely inspection in the process.

By Zeus. Constantine was *not* jealous of a dog, and by no stretch of the imagination was Gilly a *handsome boy*. Not with that tattered ear that dropped over his forehead, nor his doggy smile that rather made him appear as if he'd indulged in too much ale.

Swiveling away, Constantine raked a hand through his hair, messing the already untidy strands further. He hadn't bothered with brushing it into one of the fashionable styles the young bucks of the *ton* favored.

Embly had long since given up on Constantine's unruly, overly long hair. Keeping him reasonably shaven and presentable in unrumpled attire strained the bounds of the valet's best intentions.

At least Embly hadn't threatened to give his notice *this* week.

That was an improvement.

Constantine slid the bane of his existence a side-eyed glance.

Miss Roth would smite him to cinders if she caught him gawping at her backside.

He did not ogle or dally with his female employees. Given Mrs. Mettlebank was five and sixty if she was a day and weighed three stone more than he did, and as Miss Roth scarcely contained her disdain of him, there wasn't any desire to ogle to begin with.

He added another scientific article to the satchel upon his desk.

As Miss Roth removed her bonnet, her gaze, which never missed a detail, landed on the bulging satchel.

"Are you going somewhere, my lord?"

Folding his arms, Constantine rested his hips against the edge of the desk.

"As a matter of fact, we are."

"*We?*" She paused in drawing off her plain straw bonnet. Her dark brown eyes rounded, and her attention shifted to the bag and then back to him. "I beg your pardon. I thought you said *we*."

He grinned, delighting in flummoxing her for once.

"I did indeed, Miss Roth." He nodded and crossed his ankles. "We. You, me, Embly, Mr. Camberg-Trainer, and Gilly depart for Dovetonwick Court at first light on Tuesday."

He hadn't informed Harvey yet, and his friend might refuse, given his current infatuation. Embly would suffice as a chaperon, he supposed.

Had you hired a male amanuensis, you would not need a chaperone.

Water under the bridge.

Constantine *had* hired a female, so he must deal with the consequences.

"I..." Miss Roth swallowed as she slowly lifted the hat from her head, revealing the mass of glorious fair curls threaded with bronze, gold, and fire ribbons. Her hair betrayed her, revealing the spitfire's temperament before she opened her mouth. "*This* Tuesday?"

"I did mention when I hired you that the position involved the possibility of travel."

He'd hoped that particular detail would put her off. Traveling unescorted with a male and all that. Any sensible miss would've gone pale and promptly bid him good day.

Miss Roth had not.

Constantine quirked an eyebrow, anticipating her response.

"Yes, you did, my lord."

Remarkably composed, she hung her bonnet on the coat rack, removed her gloves, and then her deep green spencer. Today, she wore a yellow calico gown sprinkled with pastel flowers.

She appeared young and pretty and feminine.

It was the first time he could recall that she hadn't worn a severe, drab-colored frock or masculine waistcoat and skirt. He presumed she preferred severe styles and unassuming colors. The modest but tasteful gown she wore today revealed again how little he knew or understood about Miss Roth.

Folding her hands before her, she tilted her head to the side. "This is a business trip?"

"Business and pleasure." Constantine scratched his chin, the stubble beneath his fingers reminding him he ought to shave. It had been three—no, four—days. "My eldest sister is getting married."

At one and thirty, three years Constantine's senior, Charlotte had waited for true love.

"I see." A spark of defiance glinted in Miss Roth's eyes, and she set her shoulders at a recalcitrant angle. "And if I decline to accompany you?"

Clasping his hands behind him, he twisted his mouth into a wry smile.

"Sadly, Miss Roth, I would deem it grounds for termination."

"*Sadly*? I'll just bet," she murmured so softly that Constantine barely heard her.

Was this the excuse he had been looking for?

His way to rid himself of the delightfully irritating Miss Roth?

Why wasn't he thrilled at the notion then?

Because who would transcribe for him? Take precise, excellent dictation in a neat script? Organize his sloppily written notes? Straighten and organize the debacle that was his office and laboratory?

"I see," she said again, a trifle louder. Inhaling a deep breath—likely to keep from telling Constantine precisely what she thought of him—she angled toward her tidy desk. "What time should I be here?"

"No need." Straightening, Constantine waved his hand. "I'll collect you at six. Leave your direction with my coachman." He studied her from beneath half-closed eyelids. The air fairly crackled with her disapproval.

He didn't know what devil on his shoulder prompted him, but he drove the point home. "It's a three-day journey. Each way."

Miss Roth sank gracefully onto her chair and began arranging her instruments. She picked up the notes he'd left for her and, forehead puckered, perused them.

"Three days in a coach. Bloody marvelous," she muttered beneath her breath, her lips scarcely moving. "Six if you count both ways."

Her one imperfection.

Miss Roth talked to herself.

More often than naught, she murmured something unflattering about his character.

"Did you say something, Miss Roth?"

Constantine couldn't quite check his satisfied grin.

She glanced up and fashioned an insincere smile. No hint of warmth shone in the frosty stare she leveled him.

Weren't brown eyes the color of treacle supposed to be warm?

Constantine was positive she wished him to the lowest level of Hades.

"Nothing of import, my lord."

Unable to restrain his humor any longer, he chuckled, and she skewered him with those big pansy eyes.

Picking up the quill, she held it suspended. "She who laughs last laughs longest."

Quoting Shakespeare, is she?

She was full of surprises today.

Miss Faith Roth was a perplexing enigma.

"Is that a challenge, Miss Roth?"

"Heavens, no, my lord." She bent her bright head to her task. "Consider it more of a prophecy."

I hope you enjoyed this free preview of
NEVER A PROPER LADY
Secrets of Scandalous Ladies
Book Five

FROM THE DESK OF COLLETTE CAMERON®

©BLUE ROSE ROMANCE® LLC

Thank you for reading HIS ONE AND ONLY LADY. While this is a sweet Regency with inspirational overtones, I also attempted to tastefully introduce romantic elements.

I've had a few readers comment that they don't believe people can fall in love as quickly as some of my characters have done. I respect that opinion, but I don't share it. Multiple studies have been conducted that prove love at first sight is real. My husband asked me to marry him three weeks after we met. At this writing, we've been married almost 39 years.

I had a cousin whose husband asked her to marry him on their first date. They were happily married until she died of cancer 21 years later. My daughter's best friend fell in love at first sight and was married three months later. Even my own son, a true skeptic about love and marriage, fell in love with his fiancé on their first date. My grandmother told me she fell in love with my grandfather the first time she saw him. They were happily married for over 50 years. I've asked my reader group if they believe in love at first sight, and many, many of them shared their own stories.

That aside, this is a work of fiction, and magical things happen on the pages of books.

The fifth book in my Secrets of Scandalous Ladies Series is NEVER A PROPER LADY. As you might have already guessed, Faith Roth and Constantine Kellingrave's tale is an enemy to lovers romance. Yes, there will be a sixth book too!

In this book, I mention some of Purity's closest friends who were raised with her at Haven House and Academy for the Enrichment of Young Women. These are their stories if you are interested in reading the other books in the Secrets of Scandalous Ladies Series:

Joy Morrisette: A LADY'S SCANDALOUS KISS
Mercy Brockman: NO LADY FOR THE LORD
Chasity Terramier: LOVE LESSONS FOR A LADY

I have another important point I'd like to briefly touch on, which I have mentioned in all of the books in the series. Recently, a reader outside the United States became upset that I used American spellings in my Secrets of Scandalous Ladies Series, which is set in Regency England. I use American spelling in all of my Regency and Highlander series.

Multiple factors go into an author deciding which spellings to use for their books. I chose American spelling simply because most of my reading audience is American, and my books are published in America. While I stick to a few British rules, such as I shall and I shan't instead of I will and won't, I haven't extensively adopted other British grammatical rules and spelling. I believe my readers are flexible enough to adapt to slightly different spellings. After all, it's the romance novel that matters, right?

To stay abreast of the releases of the other books in the Secrets of Scandalous Ladies Series, or my other books, you can subscribe to my newsletter or visit my author world at collettecameronbooks.com.

I hope your heart was warmed by Theran and Purity's romance. If you liked their story, please consider leaving a review.

Hugs,
Collette

If you haven't joined Collette's exclusive mailing list click on QR image to sign up! You'll get access to exclusive content, sneak peeks, contests, giveaways, and more...
(P.S. No spam!)

https://collettecameronbooks.com/freegift

Collette loves to hear from readers.
You can contact her via her website: collettecameron-books.com.
Or email her directly at collette@collettecameron-books.com.

You can also follow Collette on social media:
Facebook: https://www.-facebook.com/ColletteCameronNovels/
Instagram: https://instagram.com/collettecameronauthor/
Goodreads: https://www.goodreads.com/collettecameron
Book Bub: https://www.bookbub.com/authors/collette-cameron

Giggles are Guaranteed
Collette's Cheris Reader Group

https://www.facebook.com/groups/CollettesCheris/

If you love to chat about all things romance-book related and enjoy taking part in fun and engaging live events, contests, and giveaways join **Collette's Chèris VIP Reader Group, https://www.facebook.com/groups/CollettesCheris/,** my exclusive private book group on Facebook.

Giggles are guaranteed!

Hope to see you there,
Collette Cameron®

ABOUT THE AUTHOR

USA Today Bestselling author Collette Cameron® is renowned for her captivating, humorous, and heartwarming Scottish and Regency historical romance novels. With over 65 published titles, over 1.6 million books sold around the world, and multiple writing awards to her credit, Collette is a well-known author in the world of historical romance.

Readers love her witty and relatable characters including daring rogues, dashing scoundrels, and the strong and spirited heroines who capture their hearts. From the rugged highlands to the refined drawing rooms of Regency England, Collette's novels will transport you to another time and place, where love and adventure are just a page away.

Collette's Sweet-to-Spicy Timeless Romances® are the perfect escape for readers looking for romantic escape, poignant inspiration, engaging humor, and entertaining stories.

Based in the Pacific Northwest, Collette is surrounded by the lush greenery and rainy skies that inspire her writing. She dreams of one day splitting her time between the Pacific Northwest and Scotland. In the meantime, she indulges in her love of all things cobalt blue, dachshunds, chocolate, and of course, crafting her next historical romance.

Blue Rose Romance® LLC
collette@collettecameronbooks.com
collettecameronbooks.com

BLUE ROSE ROMANCE® LLC
COLLETTE CAMERON'S® COMPLETE BOOK LIST

CHRONICLES OF THE WESTBROOK BRIDES
A Romantic Opposites Attract Mystery & Suspense
Family Saga Regency Romance

Midnight Christmas Waltz — Book 1
Mission at Midnight — Book 2
The Midnight Marquess — Book 3
Holly, Mistletoe, and Midnight Snow — Book 4
The Wallflower's Midnight Waltz— Book 5
Minuet at Midnight— Book 6
Kiss a Rake at Midnight — Book 7
Unmasked at Midnight — Book 8
Memories Made at Midnight — Book 9
Once Upon a Midnight Dream — Book 10

LADIES OF OPPORTUNITY
A Bluestockings and Rogues Opposites Attract
Regency Mystery Christmas Romance

DUKES COME CALLING
A Sensual Marriage of Convenience
Regency Historical Romance

FOR THE LOVE OF AN EARL (Wicked Earls' Club)
A Humorous Aristocrat and Wallflower
Regency Romance Adventure

Earl of Wainthorpe — Book 1
Earl of Scarborough — Book 2
Earl of Keyworth — Book 3
Earl of Renshaw — Book 4

HEART OF A SCOT
A Passionate Enemies to Lovers
Scottish Highlander Historical Mystery
Romance Adventure

To Love a Highland Laird — Book 1
To Redeem a Highland Rogue — Book 2
To Seduce a Highland Scoundrel — Book 3
To Woo a Highland Warrior — Book 4
To Enchant a Highland Earl — Book 5
To Defy a Highland Duke — Book 6
To Marry a Highland Marauder — Book 7
To Bargain with a Highland Buccaneer — Book 8
A Christmas Kiss for the Highlander — Book 9

HIGHLAND HEATHER ROMANCING A SCOT: CASTLE BRIDES

A Passionate Enemies to Lovers Second Chance Scottish Highlander Mystery Romance

Heart of a Highlander — Prequel

The Viscount's Vow — Book 1

The Highlander's Heiress — Book 2

The Earl's Enticement — Book 3

Triumph and Treasure — Book 4

Virtue and Valor — Book 5

Heartbreak and Honor — Book

Scandal's Splendor — Book 7

Passion and Plunder — Book 8

Wishes and Wonder — Book 9

A Yuletide Highlander — Book 10

SECRETS OF SCANDALOUS LADIES

A Romantic Class Difference Forced Proximity Regency Romance with Aristocrats

A Lady's Scandalous Kiss — Book 1

THE CULPEPPER MISSES
A Humorous Wallflower Family Saga
Regency Romantic Comedy

THE HONORABLE ROGUES®
A Second Chance Redeemable Rogue
and Wallflower Regency Romance